PRAISE FOR THE

Here are some of the over 100,000 five star reviews left for the Dead Cold Mystery series.

"Rex Stout and Michael Connelly have spawned a protege."

AMAZON REVIEW

"So begins one damned fine read."

AMAZON REVIEW

"Mystery that's more brain than brawn."

AMAZON REVIEW

"I read so many of this genre...and ever so often I strike gold!"

AMAZON REVIEW

"This book is filled with action, intrigue, espionage, and everything else lovers of a good thriller want."

AMAZON REVIEW

MOMMY'S LITTLE KILLER
A DEAD COLD MYSTERY

BLAKE BANNER

Copyright © 2024 by Right House

All rights reserved.

The characters and events portrayed in this ebook are fictitious. Any similarity to real persons, living or dead, is coincidental and not intended by the author.

No part of this book may be reproduced in any form or by any electronic or mechanical means, including information storage and retrieval systems, without written permission from the author, except for the use of brief quotations in a book review.

ISBN-13: 978-1-63696-022-7

ISBN-10: 1-63696-022-7

Cover design by: Damonza

Printed in the United States of America

www.righthouse.com

www.instagram.com/righthousebooks

www.facebook.com/righthousebooks

twitter.com/righthousebooks

DEAD COLD MYSTERY SERIES
An Ace and a Pair (Book 1)
Two Bare Arms (Book 2)
Garden of the Damned (Book 3)
Let Us Prey (Book 4)
The Sins of the Father (Book 5)
Strange and Sinister Path (Book 6)
The Heart to Kill (Book 7)
Unnatural Murder (Book 8)
Fire from Heaven (Book 9)
To Kill Upon A Kiss (Book 10)
Murder Most Scottish (Book 11)
The Butcher of Whitechapel (Book 12)
Little Dead Riding Hood (Book 13)
Trick or Treat (Book 14)
Blood Into Wine (Book 15)
Jack In The Box (Book 16)
The Fall Moon (Book 17)
Blood In Babylon (Book 18)
Death In Dexter (Book 19)
Mustang Sally (Book 20)
A Christmas Killing (Book 21)
Mommy's Little Killer (Book 22)
Bleed Out (Book 23)

[Dead and Buried (Book 24)](#)
[In Hot Blood (Book 25)](#)
[Fallen Angels (Book 26)](#)
[Knife Edge (Book 27)](#)
[Along Came A Spider (Book 28)](#)
[Cold Blood (Book 29)](#)
[Curtain Call (Book 30)](#)

ONE

"John—"

"Sir—"

"Twenty-one sixty-one Watson Avenue. A woman has been murdered, and I want you and Dehan to take lead."

I took a moment to scratch my ear, then said, "Sir?"

A tiny sigh at the other end of the line and the chief said, "Do I really need to repeat it, John?"

"No, sir, twenty-one sixty-one Watson Avenue, a woman has been murdered. You want us to lead. We'll go right away."

"When you're done, come and see me straightaway. It's four fifteen. I'll expect you before six."

"Yes, sir."

I hung up. Dehan had been examining the eraser on her pencil and now shifted her narrowed eyes and pensively pursed lips in my direction. Her face was a question, so I said, "We have a live, active, hot case, Dehan, where the evidence is as fresh as dew-kissed March tulips. Let us not waste a moment!"

She stood and pulled on her black leather jacket while I shrugged into my coat, and as we headed out of the station and trotted down the two shallow steps toward my ancient burgundy Jaguar, she said:

"A woman, apparently murdered in her home, just south of the Cross Bronx Expressway..."

"Twenty-one sixty-one, that places it near the overpass, by the Westchester Creek."

"And the chief wants us to take lead because...?"

I opened the driver's door and climbed in. She got in the other side, and the doors slammed like two gunshots. The big cat growled into life, and I reversed out of the lot.

"He didn't say. He just said he wants us to report to him as soon as we're done at the victim's house."

"So, either the case is important because the president's billfold was found at the scene, and only we are good enough to deal with such a sensitive case; he's taking us off cold cases and putting us on hot ones; or this case relates somehow to a cold case and he figures we may as well take it and kill however many birds with one stone."

"My money is on that one."

I pulled onto the Bruckner Boulevard and began to accelerate. Dehan was beating a tattoo on her knees.

"So, it's an MO we've seen before in one of the cold cases."

I glanced at her and frowned. "We'll be there in five minutes and we'll find out."

"There is nothing wrong, Stone, with exercising one's deductive faculties by attempting to anticipate what one is going to find in any given situation..."

"Dear me..."

"...or set of circumstances. Call it an intellectual workout."

"Fair enough."

"At this early stage of the investigation it is unlikely to be a weapon, or a suspect, or indeed a victim. What is far more likely is that it is an MO we have seen in a previous case or cases."

I smiled at her and the slightly pompous language she was using. "Makes sense."

"We can, my dear Stone, extrapolate a little further. For a

modus operandi to stick in the chief's memory to the point that he would call us in for a renewed offense, we are looking at two things: that the MO was used a number of times and the perp is therefore a serial offender, and that it is a very serious crime—as murder indeed is."

I arched both of my eyebrows very high. "A serial killer, Dehan? That is one hell of a leap."

She spread her hands and thrust out her bottom lip. "Well, now you can gloat when you prove me wrong, can't you, Mr. Stone."

Then she grinned at me and winked and I felt odd and wobbly inside. She could still do that.

I turned left onto Castle Hill and after two blocks turned onto Blackrock Avenue, to enter Watson from the west. The house was opposite the Catholic Church of the Holy Family. There were two patrol cars outside, a crime scene van, and Frank the ME's mid-'90s Jeep Cherokee. There were also a couple of uniforms, a sergeant, and a lot of tape.

I pulled up next to Frank's Jeep and we climbed out. The sky was a clear, pallid blue, but there was already the ghost of a translucent silver moon drifting above the rooftops. A chill breeze crept in and made my skin crawl. Dehan shuddered and stuffed her hands in her pockets.

The sergeant knew us and lifted the tape. He had grizzled hair turning to gray and eyes that were slightly yellow where they should be white. He didn't look surprised to see us. But then he looked like there were few things left on Earth that would surprise him. His greeting was terse.

"Detectives."

"Sergeant Musa, who called it in?"

"Benny Jackson. He's inside. He didn't exactly call it in. More like he lost his shit and went screaming to the next-door neighbor, and she called it in. A Ms. Edna Brown."

Dehan asked, "Has he said what he was doing here?"

He shook his head. "But Edna says he was a frequent visitor."

I gave a single nod that I understood the euphemism and turned to Dehan. "Okay, let's go have a look."

Sergeant Musa turned away. "It ain't pretty."

We climbed the six steps to the front porch of the two-story redbrick box. My feet were heavy, and my legs were reluctant to move. Death is unpleasant to see. Murder is horror, madness, turned banal. Dehan glanced at me, took a deep breath, and stepped through the door like a woman diving into a cold pool in January.

The entrance hall was small, no more than seven feet square, with a narrow staircase carpeted in deep burgundy climbing up the left wall, and a white door open on the right. Through it I saw a man sitting on a faded red sofa with his elbows on his knees. He was big, tall, and lean, with big hands and feet. He had dark skin and tightly curled hair, with a scraggy beard. He watched me with large, frightened eyes.

There was a uniformed cop on the door. She had the pallor of someone who has recently vomited. She jerked her head at the stairs. "In the bedroom . . ." She winced and gave her head a small shake.

I led the way up on heavy feet. A guy in a plastic suit was dusting the banisters for prints. At the top there was a small landing, also carpeted in deep burgundy. There were three doors. The one at the far end stood open and gave onto a bathroom. The walls gleamed white under a fluorescent bulb that was reflected in a partially visible mirror. The door on the left was also open, though the light was off and the drapes were closed. From the posters I could make out on the walls, the football on the chest of drawers, and the jacket hanging on the back of the chair, I figured it might be a boy's room, though it may have been a person of gender fluidity who self-identified as a boy. In a world where everything is anything, who could tell?

The door directly in front was also open. The room was full of people, all of them dressed like spacemen in hazard suits, moving slowly around a large bed. Some were crouched down, examining the floor, while others were standing, inspecting the headboard, the bedside tables, and the wardrobe.

We stepped through the doorway into insanity. On the floor, beside the bed, I noticed a small pile of discarded clothes. The bed itself appeared at first glance to have red sheets. But it was no ordinary dye that made it that color. The sheet, the duvet, and large parts of the pillows were saturated with thick blood. Lying on the sodden sheet, with the duvet tangled around her feet and legs, was a woman. Or, more accurately, what was left of a woman.

At a guess she was in her forties, on the plump side. She lay naked, her peroxide hair tangled on the soaked red pillow. Her eyes were wide with terror, staring at a ceiling that was speckled with blood. Her mouth was open. Her arms were straight down by her sides and her fingers had clawed so hard at the sheets, she had torn into the mattress beneath.

Both breasts had been removed and lay deflated and grotesque on either side of her head. A large hunting knife with a black rubber handle protruded from her lower abdomen, just above her pubic bone. Her face, at first horrific in its expression of abject terror, had been painted with a thick coat of very red lipstick and blue eyeshadow.

Frank, slightly stooped, was leaning over her, but watching us.

I heard a sniffing from beside me and turned to look at Dehan. She said:

"Lavender. Essential oil of lavender."

Frank said, "Good." Then he straightened up and stepped toward the door. "Please leave. The scene is rich. It's hard enough for us not to disturb things, and we know what we're doing."

"Rich?" I stepped closer to the head of the bed, taking care not to tread in the blood that had spilled there. I studied the twisted, agonized expression, and the exquisitely clean cut to the breast. "I don't think you're going to find a single trace of forensic evidence."

He ignored me.

"Joe's down in the kitchen. Looks like they may have been in the kitchen together having a drink or a cup of coffee before they came up here." He paused, glanced at us both in turn, and added, "I'm not that surprised to see you, to be honest. I thought the inspector might send you. I called him."

I nodded. "I can see why."

Dehan said, "The lavender, the knife in the womb, the boobs . . . What did they call him? Mommy's Boy?"

"Yeah. Five, six years ago?"

Frank stuck out his lower lip and gave his head a small shake. "It spanned a year, between 2014 and 2015. There were five that we know of, and I examined all of them. This was exactly his modus operandi. Then suddenly he just stopped."

Dehan grunted. "Looks like he just had a Kit Kat." She jerked her head at the body. "She was alive during the worst of it."

"I'm afraid so. I can tell you more when I get her back to the lab. But there are a couple of details . . ." He pointed back at the ghastly, raw wounds on her chest. "In the original killings he removed the left breast first, antemortem. As you can imagine this causes profound shock; the heart accelerates violently and the victim bleeds out very quickly. You can see there, the bleeding from the left breast is copious. However, when he removed the right breast, it was either perimortem or postmortem. There is practically no bleeding. And there is none from the knife wound."

I asked, "Who knew that, Frank? Was that ever in the news?"

He shook his head. "I knew that, my team knew, and Detective Alvarez and his team must have known, but it was never considered a fact of much relevance. Now, of course, it becomes one. The other point which might have just become relevant is the makeup."

I nodded. "I was going to talk to Joe about that . . ."

Dehan interrupted me. "We need that analyzed and compared with the makeup used in the original killings. Was it always the same?"

Frank smiled at her, but not with much humor. "Yes, that was my point. He always used the same brand and shades. L'Oréal—"

"Because she's worth it."

Frank glanced at her curiously, then went on, "All Night Blue, number six. The lipstick was British Red Three Fifty. The mascara was Age Perfect Lash Magnifying, with conditioning serum."

Dehan echoed my previous question. "And who would have known that?"

Frank shook his head. "Me, Joe, one or two guys on our teams, Alvarez. We discussed it, but the detective's attitude, and I can understand it, was that it was interesting, but it didn't really get you anywhere."

There was a derisive edge to Dehan's snort. "Well it will now. It will tell us if our perp's a copycat or the real thing."

I nodded. "And a little more than that, I hope. Frank, we'll come and see you when you have her at the lab. I want to see if Joe has anything downstairs."

Dehan led the way back down, speaking over her shoulder as she went. "In the Mommy's Boy murders they never found any forensic evidence at the scene. Alvarez never got close. Where is Alvarez now? He moved west, didn't he?"

"San Diego PD. He took a lot of flack for not solving the case."

The kitchen was part of an open-plan living room, dining room, kitchen affair with narrow French doors onto a backyard. The drapes were closed, like the drapes over the window that looked out onto Watson Avenue and the Holy Family Church. There was a small dining table down by the kitchen, with three bentwood chairs. And almost opposite the door there was a red sofa and a coffee table facing a large, flat-screen TV. Forming a nest with the sofa, there were two battered armchairs.

In and around the kitchen were Joe, the head of the crime scene team, and a couple of his guys, all dressed in plastic. On the sofa, watching us with big, frightened eyes, was the same guy I'd seen earlier. Sergeant Musa was with him, writing in a notebook. I approached.

"Benny Jackson?"

He nodded. "Yeah."

I sat in one of the armchairs, and Dehan remained standing, watching him. Musa closed his pad. "I'm done. You need me for anything?"

I told him I didn't, and he left. I said to Benny, "Tell me what happened."

He jerked his head at the door. "I just told him."

I allowed my mouth to pretend it was smiling. My eyes told him it wasn't for real. "Now tell me. As soon as you do that, you can go home."

"I come to see Claire, 'bout four o'clock. The door was open. I come in and I went upstairs . . ."

Dehan was already shaking her head. "Slow down, Benny. Let's start with how come you just went in when the door was open. You didn't knock or ring the bell?"

"No. We was friends. She often left the door open and I just come in. That weren't nothin' strange."

"Okay, so how come you didn't come in here to look for her, or the kitchen?"

He shrugged. "I called her. She din' answer, and sometimes, a lot of times, when I come to see her she's already upstairs in her room. So I just done like I always done. I went right on up."

Realization dawned. "You were having a sexual relationship with Claire?"

He screwed up his brow. "Huh?"

"You and Claire were lovers."

His slack mouth kind of sagged into a smile. "Lovers?" He grunted something like a laugh. "Yeah, right, lovers."

Dehan arched an eyebrow and folded her arms. "Are you saying she was a sex worker?"

"No, man, nothin' like that. She was a gas, we had a laugh.

Ain't nobody rich 'round here. We all need a bit of somethin', right? I give her fifty bucks sometimes and she says, come 'round, we'll have a party. That kinda thing. Claire weren't nobody's whore, man. She was a good woman. I'm gonna miss her bad."

His lips and his nose seemed to swell instantly, his eyes flooded with tears, and he wiped his whole face with his wrists.

Dehan spoke softly. "I'm sorry, Benny, I didn't know. It's gotta be tough."

He wiped his face with his sleeve now. "When I got up there and saw what I seen, I just kinda lost it. I didn't wanna see that, man, and I ran. I think I was screamin'. When I got to the front yard, Edna was on the porch saying, 'What happened? What happened? Benny, talk to me!' and I'm just screamin' like a crazy person, till I says to her, 'Call the cops, Edna! Call the cops. Claire's been hurt. She's been hurt real bad!' I din' wanna believe she was dead."

It was a simple enough story, and unless he was a thespian genius, he was telling the truth as accurately as he remembered it. I asked him, "Think carefully, Benny. When you were approaching the house, did you see anyone, did anything happen that caught your attention? Anything at all out of the ordinary?"

"Man, I was jus' thinkin' about Claire and her moves, and the party we was gonna have. I wasn't thinkin' about nothin' else. I din' see nobody nor nothin' strange at all."

Dehan said, "Cars."

He squinted at her. "What?"

"Cars. Most of the time the cars parked outside houses in residential areas are the same cars, in pretty much the same places at the same times." He thought about it a second and shrugged. She went on. "Think back. Were they the same cars?"

"Maybe . . ." He paused. "You know? Now you say it, maybe, there was an old-model cream Ford SUV, maybe a Kuga? Maybe, 'cross the way, outside the church."

I sucked my teeth for a moment, then sighed and nodded. "Okay, Benny. You can go. On your way out tell Sergeant Musa about the car so he can add it to your statement. Show him where you saw it."

He got to his feet and walked out of the room, rubbing the back of his head with his huge hand and sobbing quietly as he went.

TWO

Joe had told us he would have nothing for us until he'd finished and got back to the lab, so we went next door to Edna Brown's house. Dusk was turning to evening and the cold air had developed an icy bite. Edna was at her bow window, peering through her drapes with the warm light of her living room behind her. When she saw us enter her front yard and climb the steps, she left the window and hurried to the door. It opened as Dehan reached for the bell.

"I saw yous coming," she said, and offered us an uncertain smile.

I offered her a certain one and said, "We saw you see us. May we come in?"

She stood back, and the light from her hall illuminated her face. She was in her seventies, with very white skin and pink cheeks. "Is it true? Is Claire dead?"

Dehan answered. "I'm afraid so, Edna. Can you tell us anything?"

Her house was the mirror of Claire's. We had the stairs on our right, and to the left there was a door open onto a cozy, well-kept living room. She didn't answer Dehan but turned her back and tottered away toward the living room, where a gold Dralon velvet sofa and two chairs set about a coffee table echoed the shabbier setup in Claire's house. She sat on the corner of the sofa and watched us take the chairs, with her hands placed neatly on her lap.

"Poor Claire. She did struggle so. It's a cruel, hard life in this country unless you are a ruthless predator. Bless her, Claire was anything but that. She had a big heart and a weak disposition." She closed her eyes and gave her head a single shake. "And a *chronic* need for cash."

Dehan shot me a smile. "What are you trying to tell us, Edna?"

Edna smiled at her and blinked a few times. "Please, call me Mrs. Brown. I do so despise the modern lack of formality, and unless I am very much mistaken, we have not been introduced before." She sailed on seamlessly. "I am not *trying* to tell you anything. It's quite simply that poor Claire had to make ends meet, and when faced with poverty most of us do what we are good at. Some of us invest in the stock market, others turn to hydroponics and grow marijuana in the basement, while others resort to the world's oldest profession and sell sexual favors to men who are too ugly to get them in the usual manner."

I gave a small laugh and decided that I liked Mrs. Brown. "Are you skilled in hydroponics, Mrs. Brown?"

She gave a charming giggle. "Oh, dear me! You'll need a court order to find that out, and as you are Homicide and not Vice, I doubt you'll bother. Besides, no judge in this city will grant one on the basis of my whimsical passing comment. What were we talking about? You want me to tell you what happened."

"Please."

She sighed and slipped her hands between her knees. "Benny was a frequent visitor at Claire's house. They were fond of each other. She wouldn't sleep with just anyone." She frowned and shook her head. "She wasn't what you'd call a *whore*, as such. She was a party animal. She *loved* to laugh and dance and sing. She could drink most people under the table and still dance a jig around the room without falling over. Many a New Year's Eve we have partied in her house and mine until the sun has risen on a brand-new January.

"And her customers were gleaned from her friends." She wagged a finger at us. "Not her acquaintances, mind! Her *friends*. And Benny, for all that he is an ignorant dopehead, he is also kind and sensitive, and he would remember to buy her flowers from time to time, and never had to be reminded that it was her birthday. So he knew that she was hard up, and he would give her one or two hundred dollars a month. In exchange he would visit her whenever his appetite got the better of his ED."

Dehan frowned. "ED?"

"Erectile dysfunction. In a man of Benny's age, who drinks and smokes as much as he does, a little soldier who stands to attention on demand is something between a forlorn hope and a distant memory."

She leaned back with her hands clamped tightly between her knees, her cheeks glowing bright pink against her white skin, and giggled silently with her eyes screwed up tight.

Dehan smiled at me and raised her eyebrows high. When Mrs. Brown had stopped giggling, she asked her, "Did she have that kind of arrangement with many other men?"

"Oh, indeed, yes. At least four besides Bobby. The house was hers, left to her by her late husband, Earl. She figured she needed at least two thousand dollars a month. She had a part-time job at the Blueberry Café where she made about three hundred a week. So she supplemented that with what she made from these five gentlemen friends, each paying between one and two hundred dollars a month. She must have pulled in another seven hundred. I can't tell you all their names, but I know she had a diary in which she had their names and telephone numbers, so she could keep track of who was coming and when. It was a very convenient arrangement for everybody." She paused a moment in abstracted thought. "She was a terribly attractive woman: pretty, but above all with a very attractive, happy, bubbly personality. You couldn't help loving her."

I thought of the tragic, grotesque figure next door, goggling at the ceiling, soaked in her own blood.

"So, what happened today, Mrs. Brown?"

Her skin became pasty, and she averted her eyes toward her French doors and the gray light outside. She gave a small sigh through her nose.

"Today . . . We were supposed to have coffee this morning, at eleven. She didn't show. She was usually punctual and usually showed up when we made arrangements, but you know how it is with bubbly people, sometimes they get involved in things and they forget, especially if you happen to be an old woman. However, Claire and I did meet three or four times a week for coffee, usually here, and she usually showed up. We had fun gossiping and chatting."

She paused, and I saw the glisten of tears in her eyes, and the small muscle in her jaw jumping. After a moment she took a deep breath and continued.

"This morning she didn't show, and to be honest I thought nothing of it. At about twelve noon I did notice a man leaving. I am not sure I would be able to describe him. I saw him from the back, and he was very average. Perhaps a little below six foot, neither fat nor thin, jeans, I think, or chinos, and a jacket which may have been some kind of anorak. It was green or blue, at that end of the color spectrum. It wasn't red or yellow or anything like that. I simply chalked it down as the reason why she hadn't turned up and thought nothing more of it, until this afternoon, shortly after four.

"I was just settling down to read a book, *Murder on the Golf Links*, not one of her best, when I heard this unearthly noise, like the wailing of a host of banshees. It made my skin go cold and the hair on the back of my neck stand up. I ran to the window and I saw poor Benny practically fall down the steps into the yard. He was screaming and pulling at his hair and staggering around in circles. Well, I rushed out to see what was the matter with the poor man and I couldn't believe it. He said, 'Call the cops, Edna! Call the cops! Claire's been hurt. She's been hurt real bad! I think she's dead!' I'll never forget those words as long as I live."

I nodded and glanced at the bow window a moment, thinking back to what Benny had said. "Mrs. Brown, think carefully. When your nondescript visitor left this morning, did you notice if he got into a car?"

"Yes." She nodded. "Now that you mention it, he got into a white Ford SUV. It was parked across the road, down a bit toward the church."

I exchanged a glance with Dehan. "How about this afternoon, when you went out to talk to Benny, did you notice anything or anyone unusual?"

She took a deep breath and puffed out her cheeks. "I would *really* not like to say. I was not paying attention to anything, and I might invent something that didn't really happen. You know how unreliable memory can be. The SUV might have been there again, but equally it might not."

"We are nearly done, Mrs. Brown. I have just one last question. Did Claire ever mention anyone, perhaps one of her clients or anybody else, who threatened her, or made her feel threatened or afraid? Did she ever mention being followed, stalked . . ." I spread my hands. "Anything of that sort?"

She became very serious, biting her top lip, lost in thought for a moment. Then she frowned.

"There was someone. It was a couple of months ago. A man who had heard from a friend of a friend of a friend, you know how it goes, that Claire had this arrangement with Benny and a few others. This character wanted in. She agreed to meet him, but she didn't like him and she told him no. I remember she told me he scared her. She said he came on too strong. She said he had violent eyes, and that phrase stuck in my mind. He came to the house. I don't know how he got her address, must have been from one of the boys, but he came around and threatened her. She threatened him right back, she was like that. She threatened him with the police and she told him she had friends who would take care of her. He went away and didn't come back."

Dehan asked, "That was a couple of months ago?"

"Yes, six or eight weeks, more or less."

"Did she get a name?"

"Yes . . ." She sighed again, searching her memory. "It was an odd name, he may have been French. I know he was foreign. Napoleon? Are Frenchmen really called Napoleon? I'm sorry I can't be more helpful. It was something like that."

"Don't worry." I stood, and Dehan stood with me. "One of the boys will know. Thank you for your help, Mrs. Brown."

She stood too and clenched her hands in front of her. Her face twisted suddenly with anxiety.

"What will become of her son?"

Dehan stated matter-of-factly, "She had a son."

"Oscar. He's sixteen. This will destroy him."

"Where is he?"

"When she had guests he stayed with a friend of hers, Begonia. I have the number . . ."

Dehan made the call to social services and then to Begonia. Arrangements were made to pick the boy up and take him into care and assign him a caseworker, and fifteen minutes later Edna Brown led us to the door and let us out into the cold night. Claire's body, now empty and beyond pain, camouflaged within a body bag, was being loaded into the back of an ambulance whose red-and-white lights pulsed a bleak, silent dirge against the side of the church. There was a chill, metallic rattle as the gurney folded its legs, and the body was swallowed by the black maw of the vehicle. Then suddenly Claire was gone. Absently, half in a trance, I found myself reciting:

"'Fear no more the lightning flash, nor the all-dreaded thunder stone; fear not slander, censure rash; thou hast finished joy and moan: all lovers young, all lovers must, consign to thee, and come to dust.'"

Dehan watched the doors of the ambulance slam closed and the guys climb aboard. Then it pulled away, toward Castle Hill Avenue, its siren wailing like it was on an urgent mission to save a life.

"What was that?" she asked and shuddered.

"Shakespeare, 'Fear no more the heat o' the sun,' from *Cymbeline*."

"It's sad."

I made the noise of thinking then sighed. "The final verse is happier. It's an incantation to protect the grave and the departed soul. 'No exorciser harm thee! Nor no witchcraft charm thee! Ghost unlaid forbear thee! Nothing ill come near thee! Quiet consummation have; and renowned be thy name!'"

She blinked at me a few times. Her mouth smiled but her eyes were having no part of it. "She could have done with a bit of that before she got murdered."

"No argument there, Dehan. No argument there. Come on, let's go see the chief."

We made our way in silence to the burgundy beast, and I slipped behind the wheel. The big cat roared, and I pulled away, back toward the 43rd. The streetlamps passed in a steady procession. I glanced at Dehan, silent beside me, and the light from the lamps and the passing, illuminated shop fronts bathed her face with alternating light and shadow.

She spoke suddenly, without looking at me. "So Mommy's Boy is back. What do you think, he's been away, killing somewhere else, and now he's back in town? Or he went into a kind of psychotic remission and now the urge is back?"

I thought about it for a moment, seeing the bed, soaked in brilliant red blood, and Claire's ghastly face gaping at the ceiling.

"I think it's too soon to say. We need to go through the old cases, and if possible talk to Alvarez, see what he remembers, what feelings he had. We also need to hear what Joe has to say about the makeup."

"Sure, but the lavender oil, and the sequence of the cuts, only a handful of people knew that."

I nodded once. "That much is true."

"So it has to be him."

"Maybe. Let's gather information first before we come to any conclusions."

"You think I'm jumping to conclusions?"

She still didn't look at me. I waited a moment and shook my head.

"No. There was a hell of a lot of information there. Too much to process straightaway. Some of it we haven't got yet. We need time to collate it, sift through it, and see what makes sense and what doesn't."

I glanced at her. She was still staring out of the windshield, but by the dim glow of the passing lights I could see there were tears on her cheeks. I didn't say anything. I reached over and held her hand with mine. She squeezed it, and we made the rest of the short journey in silence.

THREE

Inspector John Newman watched us sit down, chewing his lip, and when we were comfortable lowered himself into his own chair.

"You will both have gathered why I want you to take lead on this case."

Dehan answered. "Yes, sir. It appears to be the Mommy's Boy killer, which became a cold case about five years back, when the killings stopped abruptly."

He observed her a moment from under his brows, then turned to me. "It stuck in my craw when that case went cold. Even if you weren't working the cold cases, I want you on that bastard's tail. I want you to hound him, sniff him out, and nail him to the wall. I am only sorry we have abolished the death penalty, John, because, may God forgive me, creatures like that do not deserve to live. I'm sorry, forgive me for expressing myself so frankly, Carmen. John, you are the best detective at the Forty-Third, and Carmen, you come a damned close second. I want you to find this son of a bitch, and I want you to eliminate him."

He held my gaze, and it was like the sheer power of his will was holding me, driving me to understand what he was communicating with his eyes, because the words were forbidden. The moment became surreal as it dawned on me what he was asking me to do. I scowled at him.

"Sir?"

He leaned forward with his elbows on his desk. The mild, amiable facade was gone. His eyes were hard, ruthless, and his mouth was an unrelenting line. The Bronx kid who'd fought his way up through the ranks before quotas and positive discrimination glared back at me and snarled.

"John, what he does to those women, he does while they are alive. They bleed out, but before they bleed out they go into shock from the sheer, unendurable horror of what he is doing to them. These are good, decent women struggling to raise their kids in a society that does not care about them. And this *bastard* breaks into their homes and visits pain and horror on them that we cannot even conceive; we cannot begin to *imagine*! And do you know what will happen when you arrest him and bring him to justice?"

"Sir, I am not sure I am following..."

"He will be prosecuted and he will be convicted because you are both damned good cops. And when he gets to Southport or Attica, he will then be *protected* from the other inmates by the prison staff. He will be urged to educate himself, better himself, he will see a psychologist and be encouraged to take up watercoloring, or creative writing. Maybe he'll even write his autobiography and become a millionaire!"

The silence that followed seemed to ring against the walls.

"Sir." I hesitated for just a moment. "Is there a personal issue here? I have to ask, because if there is..."

He shook his head. "No. There is no personal issue here, John. I was briefly involved in the original investigation. I saw firsthand what he did to the first two victims, how he killed them, and I watched how Detective Alvarez, who was a damned good cop, don't get me wrong, but I watched how he danced to this bastard's tune while woman after woman was tortured to death by this... *monster!* Alvarez never stood a chance. This bastard played him like a violin. What we need here is for you, both of you, to get inside his skin, get inside his mind"—he stabbed at his head with his finger—"and get a step ahead of him. He cannot be allowed to kill again—*ever!* Find him, John, and *stop* him!"

I hesitated again. "Sir, when you say stop him. We will find him and arrest . . ."

Dehan interrupted me. "We have the file, sir. We're going to take it home and go through it with a fine-tooth comb. We'll get inside his skin, and we will stop him, sir."

He stared at her awhile, then smiled and nodded. "I believe you will. I believe you will, Carmen."

We made our way down the stairs to the detectives' room. We now had a couple of steel filing cabinets for the cold cases, which had replaced the cartons we had started out with, and we worked our way through the approximate alphabetical order until we found the Mommy's Boy case. It was thick and detailed. We shared out the contents and started to read.

After a while, Dehan went and got two paper cups of coffee-like liquid. When she returned, she placed one in front of me, dropped into her chair, and crossed her boots on the corner of her desk. Then she started to talk as she leafed through the pages.

"There were five victims, Claire Carter makes six. The first was on the first of January, 2014. Mary Campbell, black, forty-five years old, murdered in her home in her bedroom. She was a single mother and had one son who was not at home at the time. Testimony from friends said that she was not a professional prostitute, but did see men and took money from them."

She tossed me some photographs. Some were of the crime scene and were strikingly similar to the scene we had just come from, the only difference being that Claire had been white, and Mary Campbell had been African American. There were a couple more photographs where she was smiling into the camera. She was slightly overweight, attractive, and seemed to smile easily.

Dehan was talking again. "The second, on the fifth of May, 2014, Maria Ortiz, Puerto Rican, thirty-eight years old, mother of four, one boy and three girls, murdered at home in her bedroom while the kids were staying with their aunt. She was a widow. Again, she saw men and received money, but did not have a pimp and didn't walk the streets."

She tossed over another set of photographs. I clipped the first lot together with a makeshift label and looked at Maria Ortiz. She was pretty, with a bright smile, slightly overweight. The crime scene was again identical in all significant details, except that Maria was Latina, neither black nor Caucasian. I clipped the pictures together and labeled them.

Dehan moved on. "Third, Olga Hernandez, hazard a wild guess at the date."

I glanced at the first two, studied her face a moment, and said, "Tenth of October?"

"Give the man a peanut. She was Colombian, forty-eight years old, and the single mother of one boy. Like the others, she was a dilettante lady of the night."

The pictures seemed to conform to the emerging pattern. She was slightly overweight, pretty, smiling, suggesting a sunny disposition. The crime scene was, at a glance, the same. I labeled them as I listened to Dehan.

"So we have one Afro-American, two Latinas, and now Sharon Lipschitz, Jewish, a nurse, mother of three boys and one girl, murdered, like the others, in her bedroom, while her husband was at work and the kids were at school. Friends were adamant that she was a respectable, faithful housewife. Unthinkable that she might be on the game. Take a shot at the date, Stone."

"Third of March, 2015. Every five months."

I examined the pictures. Sharon was pretty, like the others. The photographs showed her laughing, smiling, bright. The crime scene was as the others.

Dehan sighed. "Finally, Margaret Allen, white, divorced mother of one boy and one girl. No known connection with prostitution, dilettante or otherwise. Murdered, like the others, in her bedroom, while the kids were at school. Take a shot at the date."

She looked up and raised an eyebrow. I drew breath but stopped short. "Not the eighth of August 2015."

She shook her head. "Third of January."

"Son of a bitch."

She tossed me the pictures. Again, she was bright, pretty, laughing, and the crime scene was identical. I clipped them and labeled them while I spoke.

"He knows the cops are going to look for patterns of behavior to try and profile him, so he creates patterns and then breaks them. Dates, kids, race, prostitution, sexual morality—he doesn't give a damn about any of it."

Dehan was nodding slowly. "The only constants are that the women are slightly overweight, and, from witness statements and the photographs, they all seem to have been happy, lively, and friendly."

"Possibly a soft touch for a predator. But here's the brilliant part of his strategy: we don't know if these are constants at all. They are simply what has remained constant so far."

She banged her fist gently on the desk. "So is Claire Carter part of this strategy? Or has he just been away killing out of state, with a completely different MO?"

"We don't know." I sat forward and laid both hands on the desk. "That, Dehan, is the first thing that we need to get to grips with. He is smart, and what we know about him is practically zero. This is what the chief was talking about. He played Alvarez like a violin. Had him chasing a profile that was all smoke and mirrors and did not actually exist."

"Jesus . . . !"

"We need to set up a board where we can build profiles of the victims and of suspects, and we are going to need a team to do the donkey work. But first we are going to need to take this home and digest it. Because there is one thing we *can* be sure of. All this misdirection and smoke and mirrors is designed to conceal something. And that something is there to be concealed. Note: one, he kills women, and all the elaborate trickery is *for the purpose* of enabling him to kill women. Two, he cuts off the left breast so that the victim bleeds to death. The left breast is over the heart, the source of life and love. This, you can stake my career and my reputation on it, is as central to his urge to kill as is killing women. All the rest of it may be show, but the need to kill women and remove their left breast, those are central and integral to his homicidal drive."

She nodded a lot. Then raised her right hand with her index finger erect, while still nodding. "And there is one more thing, Stone. It doesn't stand out, it's actually almost buried under all the other details. Every one of the victims has had at least one son."

I thought about it. "Yeah, I am no psychologist, as you once pointed out to me, but two gets you twenty that in his mind the boy—the victim's son—represents him; *is* him."

"Yeah, you're probably right. We need to get an FBI profiler in and get some idea about who we're chasing here."

"Agreed."

We sat in silence awhile, looking at each other. She seemed suddenly small and very vulnerable. I smiled at her.

"You've never been on one of these before?"

She shook her head. "No."

"It's harrowing, and it never gets any easier. But"—I shrugged —"you build up defenses. You learn to deal with it somehow."

"I need a drink."

"Okay, let's get this stuff home. We'll order in pizza and a bottle of wine."

"Pizza?" She screwed up her face. "I'll try, but I might just stick to tequila." She swung her feet off the desk and sat forward. "Did Alvarez have anyone in his sights? Was there *anyone* of interest?"

"Yeah." I stood and pulled my coat off the back of my chair, then picked up the file and leafed through it. "James Campbell . . ."

She frowned. "Campbell? Any relation to the first victim?"

"Mary Campbell, yeah, her son. Alvarez's notes say he is a minister in a religious mission on Castle Hill and Homer. He says he displays signs of being seriously misogynistic and perhaps a religious fanatic. However, he was unable to link him to the other murders and never had enough to try and get a psych evaluation."

She leaned back. "He's got to be worth a visit. The first victim's son, and all the victims have sons . . . ?"

I nodded and kept reading. "There was also a Nelson Vargas, known to be a member of the Cabras gang. Rap sheet as long as your arm, but no serious charges made to stick, suspected of several murders, mostly gang related, rape, dealing . . ." I shook my head as I read. "You name it."

"How's he connected to this?"

"Maria Ortiz called the cops five days before she was killed and complained that he had threatened her with rape and murder. Ring a bell?"

I glanced at her. She said, "Claire made the same complaint. We need to find out if it's the same guy. Anyone else come on Alvarez's radar?"

"Yeah, he had no trouble finding suspects, just making it stick. George Allen, Margaret Allen's ex-husband. That's the last victim before he went off the radar."

"That's odd." I looked at her. She was frowning. "It just feels wrong. You'd expect her to be the first. He kills her and gets a taste for it. Not to start killing strangers and then kill his own wife. It feels wrong."

I made a "what can I tell you?" face and read on.

"He's the sales director of SuperWare, a company that develops and produces supermarket software."

"Supermarket software?"

"Sales director. You don't need to be a genius, but you do need to be smart and a strategist. He moved to Rochester five years ago, shortly before the killings stopped."

She grunted, and I turned a page.

"Last one, Golam Heitz."

"Golam Heitz? Are you kidding me?"

"Nope, and get this, he was an orderly at the same hospital where Sharon Lipschitz was a nurse, the St. Barnabas, Third Avenue, in West Bronx, near the zoo. Alvarez didn't like him. His notes have him as, and I quote, 'Neurotic nerd, arrogant, spotty, thinks he's a genius, could use a bath.'" I closed the folder. "That's it. No other suspects showed up, and the main problem, according to his notes, was connecting any one of the suspects to all the murders. They are all more or less loosely connected to at least *one* of the murders, but none is linked, however tenuously, to *all* of them."

She nodded, sniffed, and sat looking around the room, now largely empty and partially dark. I pulled on my coat, but she didn't move. She said, "None is, that's correct, right? Not 'none are'?"

"Yes, Dehan, 'none is' is correct. Shall we go?"

She sighed and stood and pulled on her jacket. "I guess it used to have an apostrophe, right?"

We crossed the room and headed out into the frosty night. The billows of condensation from her breath glowed in the lamplight, and across the road a layer of white frost lay across the roof of my ancient Jaguar. She looked up at me and blinked, and I was possessed by a powerful need to protect her and care for her. She said:

"After the first 'n': 'n' apostrophe, 'one.'"

I frowned. "What?"

"Not one is, 'n' apostrophe 'one' is, 'none is.' Right?"

I laughed. "You're nuts."

"Take me somewhere you can hug me that the cops won't see us."

We made our way carefully down the steps and across the slippery blacktop toward my car, and home.

FOUR

Next morning a watery sun touched broken clouds with damp amber and liquid blue as we made our way down Castle Hill Avenue, in search of the Church of the Holy Father and Son at the End of Days.

Dehan was hiding puffy eyes behind mirrored aviators, leaning back in her seat.

"He couldn't come up with a long name, so he went for something short and pithy."

I smiled. "It covers the basics. It's a church and it is dedicated to the Holy Father and the Holy Son. He is not interested in the Holy Ghost or the Virgin Mary. And as far as he is concerned, we are approaching the end of days."

"Partying with this guy has got to be a blast."

"I read up about him while you were snoring on the sofa, cradling a glass of tequila in your hand."

"I am in awe."

She didn't sound like she meant it. "He got his degree in theology from the University of New York, then went on to Dunwoodie but dropped out after his first year and started preaching the word, as he heard it, wherever he could persuade people to listen to him. Apparently he was good at persuading, because after just two years he had gathered sufficient donations and pledges to buy a lot with a condemned building on it and start construction of his own church. He is described variously as a firebrand, a visionary, a charismatic prophet for the new age, and a dangerous charlatan.

"He has been condemned several times by black activists for not championing black rights, and he is universally reviled by women's groups and PC activists generally for his stance on women and women's rights."

She turned her head to look at me, but all I could see was myself looking back at me in her shades.

"Why don't we let him tell you that? We're here."

I spun the wheel, and we rolled into Homer Avenue, then turned right and pulled into the parking lot at the back of the church. We climbed out and stood looking at the vast, modern structure for a while. Dehan spoke my thoughts.

"That's a hell of a lot of donations in two years of preaching."

"I wonder who he was preaching to."

"Not the choir, Stone, that's for sure. I detect the subtle aroma of the laundromat."

We made our way to the front of the building. It had a beige facade with plate glass doors and a large, burgundy awning that made it look like an Italian restaurant, or a casino. We pushed through into a large, airy room with polished wooden floors, high white ceilings, and walls that were part bare brick and part pine tongue and groove. In the wall opposite us there were heavy, walnut double doors with brass handles, and above them a vast statue of a bearded man who was presumably Jesus, though he looked more Nordic than Jewish. He wore a white robe and held his arms wide in a gesture of welcome that was evocative of the cross, though there was no bleeding from injuries to his hands or feet, or his side.

Under the statue was a single wooden plaque that read, "Chapel." We crossed the echoing antechamber and pushed through the walnut doors into a large chapel, carpeted in bloodred with rows of blond wood benches facing a white, semi-circular stage with no altar, but a vast, stylized white cross that tapered into points at the end of each pole, making it look more like a star than a cross.

At the foot of the stage there was a table draped with a white linen cloth and a man in a black soutane bending over the table, stacking a large pile of books. He stood erect and turned as we came in. He was black, in his early thirties, handsome, lean, and angry. At a glance I guessed that the man smiling reassuringly on the cover of the books he was holding was himself.

We started down the aisle toward him and I said, "Reverend James Campbell?"

The acoustics in the room were good, and my voice echoed loudly. His voice was louder and deeper.

"That is I. Who, then, are you?"

I pulled my badge and sensed Dehan do the same beside me. "Detective John Stone, of the NYPD. This is my partner, Detective Carmen Dehan."

He grazed her with his eyes as we drew level with him, and curled his lips.

"Where are your children, woman?"

I felt Dehan stiffen and spoke quickly. "Detective Dehan has no children, Reverend. We'd like to ask you some questions."

He didn't answer for a moment, but remained scrutinizing Dehan, then shifted insolent eyes onto me. "About what, Detective?"

"About your mother."

"My mother was a whore of Babylon and was struck down and removed hence to hell as all whores will be when judgment comes. She is of no importance. Nothing. She served her purpose as an organ of birth to bring me forth as a crusader for the Father. Now she is gone."

"That's pretty harsh." I reached out and picked up one of his books, looked at his posed, grinning form on the cover, and turned it over to look at the back. "What did she do to earn the label 'whore'?"

"She fornicated! She fornicated freely and of her own free will. She fornicated with men and boys alike without restraint, and for coin. She transgressed the most sacred of the Father's laws. She was a harlot!"

I managed a frown and a smile at the same time. "The most sacred of the Father's laws? I assume you are talking about Jehovah?"

"What other Holy Father do you know of, Detective?"

I sat on the front pew and placed his book on my lap. "None, but I don't recall any of the Ten Commandments saying anything about promiscuity. Number one states, in true Judeo-Christian fashion, that the faithful shall have no other god but Him. Two outlaws graven images, and three is an admonition not to take the Lord's name in vain. Four was to remember the Sabbath and keep it holy, and five"—I paused to wag a finger at him—"admonished us to honor thy father *and* thy mother. We don't get to though shalt not kill till number six. Seven enjoins us not to commit adultery but says nothing of consensual premarital sex. Eight tells us not to steal, nine not to bear false witness, and ten bids us not to covet. Nothing there about being promiscuous or selling sexual services."

He had gone very still. His eyes were venomous.

"You quote the Old Testament at me?"

I shrugged my eyebrows. "The most sacred of the Father's laws? Where else would you find them but in the Ten Commandments?"

Suddenly he was bellowing, "*The Bible is nothing but a pack of Jewish lies! A fabrication by the church of the Antichrist and Nicea! Open your eyes and see the truth! Open your mind and your heart to the truth of the Lord!*"

I raised my left hand while still looking down at the book on my lap. "Thank you, Reverend, but what I would really like to know is, what is this sacred law you are speaking about? Where did it come from?"

"*It came from the Father!*"

"But how did you find it? How did *you* come by it? Where is it written?"

He narrowed his eyes and studied me for so long I thought he wasn't going to answer. Finally he gave a small cough and spoke quietly.

"The Father spoke to me. He opened my eyes and poured clear light into my mind and my heart, so that I was able of a sudden clearly to see the lies which beguile and blind the minds of men!"

Dehan took a seat on the far side of the aisle. He didn't seem to notice her. "When was that?"

I made a point of not sounding confrontational, but intelligently interested. He picked up a copy of his own book and laid his palm on it.

"She was killing me, the harlot, grinding me down day by day, driving steel blades into my soul, twisting them, plunging them deeper, ripping me apart and laughing, laughing, always laughing! Every day I came home from school to hear her upstairs, the grotesque, animal noises, the cheap creaking of the whore's bed, the grunting of the animals she took there, and her incessant, eternal, *damned* laughing!

"I prayed. The Father knows I prayed. I implored Him to set me free from that hell. I prayed for Him to liberate me from my own hatred, to view her with His own dispassionate compassion. But He ignored me."

"He ignored you?"

He nodded heavily. "He ignored me, because one of the greatest lies that the Judeo-Satanic Bible tells is that we must learn to forgive." He leaned forward and shrieked, "*We must never forgive! Never! Never! Never forgive!*"

He walked away on long, slow legs, then stopped and looked

up at the ceiling. His voice was like the disembodied howl of an imprisoned daemon.

"*We must punish!*"

He didn't turn to face me. He remained staring at the ceiling above him and bellowed again, "*Lord Father! Give me strength! We must punish!*"

Then he turned slowly to face me, and his eyes slewed toward Dehan.

"He made me see. The original sin was not Adam and Eve's disobedience of the Father. *It was the creation of Eve!*"

"The creation of Eve? God committed the original sin?"

"*No! Imbecile! Fool! Do you not see? Yet the Father gave you eyes! It was Satan! Satan who created Eve from Adam's rib! For woman is the spawn of Satan!*"

He was silent, panting, like he'd been running a long distance. After a moment I said, "Oh, I see . . ."

"Do you? All evil that has ever befallen Man has come from woman. We were created in the Father's holy image! But tell me, answer me this, is there a queen of Heaven? Is there a Holy Mother? Has Jesus a sister? No! Nay! Nay! Nay to this! Man, *man* was made in the Father's image! Has the Father breasts? Has the Father a *cunnus*? No? Then in *what way*—tell me—in what way are *they* made in the image of the Father? *Tell me that!* They are the spawn of Satan! He created him and they are his servants! Sent to the Garden to lure Adam to his perdition."

"And the Father told you this?"

"Yes."

"Does he often speak to you?"

"Don't patronize me, Detective Stone. The Father does not speak to me. He gave me Grace of understanding. He infused my mind and my heart with His grace and His truth, and I understood."

"What did you understand, Reverend?"

"That the creation of women was the true original sin that brought the downfall of Man. That woman is inherently evil, and that the lascivious hunger for sex will destroy us. The only way to salvation for Man is to eliminate women from the face of the Earth."

I leaned forward with my elbows on my knees and frowned at him.

"Really?"

He pointed at me with outstretched arm. "You know, in your heart, that I am right. You can *feel* the truth of my words. You *know* that the Father speaks through me."

"Was it that clarity that led you to know that you had to kill the whore?"

He barked a loud laugh. "I did not kill the whore. The Father freed me. He sent another with that sacred task and set me free."

"He sent another? Do you know whom he sent?"

He shook his head. "It is of no moment, Detective, for the primary purpose was served, which was to liberate me and allow me to bring the true word to the people!"

I smiled. "Reverend Campbell, your mother was murdered."

"Do you not listen? What do I need to do to bring clarity to your mind? Do you send out detectives every time a swine is slaughtered in an abattoir? Every time a chicken is slaughtered or a rat is exterminated? Then why trouble when a woman is killed? She is lower on the scale of life value than the rat or the cockroach, for where they are dumb vermin, she is *evil*! She carries Satan's seed and his intent!"

"Reverend Campbell, do you know who killed your mother?"

"No! And I don't care! I have told you it is of no consequence!"

"A jury might think otherwise if you are tried for conspiracy to murder, or aiding and abetting a murderer."

He smiled at me and shook his head. "I stand before a higher court than you, Detective, and I have no fear of your mundane games. Do what you must do, the Father will be my guide."

"Where were you the night your mother was murdered?"

"I was out, visiting with friends. Your detectives asked me all this at the time. The Father intervened and removed me from the house . . ."

I snapped, "But you were still living at home with your mother."

"I was a prisoner! Yes, indeed! What of it? I already told you the Father set me free! *The Father set me free!*"

"What time did you get home?"

He turned his back on me and gazed up at the huge cross.

"I walked through that door, that open door, at exactly twelve o'clock at night. I went into the living room, where we had the dinner table, and I saw the fire was cold in the grate. I saw there was no food cooked. I was not dismayed, for this is a woman. This is what we may expect from their slovenly, deceitful species. I went upstairs to berate her and give her the sharp edge of my tongue, and what I found was judgment. Judgment had been visited upon her, without pity and without compassion. And that was the moment."

"What moment?"

"That was the moment that the Father gave me His holy grace and made me understand. He had punished her for transgressing against His most sacred law."

I nodded, trying to collate what he was telling me, to give it shape in my mind.

"What is that most sacred law, Reverend Campbell?"

"Women! Women must not engage in sexual intercourse. Women must never engage in coitus. Nor in any kind of sexual activity."

"It is okay for men?"

"It is not a sin for men. It should be resisted, but it is not a sin."

"Only a sin if women do it. That is going to make it pretty hard for the race to procreate."

He gave me that kind of kindly patronizing look fathers give their sons when they are being particularly stupid.

"That is kind of the point, Detective Stone. Once the race

starts to die out, because men have the strength to resist the lure and temptation of women, then the Father will grant us final salvation. The vile species of womankind will be wiped out, and Man will rise to his preordained position, at the right hand of the Almighty Father." He paused. "Now tell me this, Detective Stone, do I need a lawyer? Do you plan to arrest me?"

I shook my head. "We were simply seeking your help and your cooperation."

"Then get the hell out of my church, and take your filthy whore bitch with you! I have no help to offer you but the light of the Holy Father. Sinners and fornicators, get the *hell* out of my church!"

I stood and showed him the book I had taken. "May I?"

He curled his lip. "Sixteen bucks."

I paid up, and we left.

FIVE

My cell rang. I paused to pull it from my pocket, and Dehan, battered by the wind blustering in off the East River, rested her ass on the hood of the Jaguar and watched me.

It was the precinct. I said, "Yeah, Stone."

"Hey gorgeous, it's your favorite sergeant."

"Hello, Maria."

"You got a witness who saw something last night at Claire Carter's house. He wants to come in and talk to you. I have him on the line now. Name's Oliver Smith."

"Thanks, Maria. Get a time from him. Soon as he can. We'll be right over."

"Hold the line, handsome." There was silence for ten seconds, then Maria came back on the line. "He'll be here in about half an hour."

"We're on our way."

I hung up. Dehan said, "Who? When? We're on our way where?"

"We have a witness. Oliver Smith. Claims he saw something yesterday. He's coming in. He'll be at the station in half an hour."

She gave me a thumbs-up and climbed in the car. I took Lafayette and then Soundview and turned onto Story Avenue ten minutes later. We had time to grab some coffee, and Maria buzzed me to let me know Oliver Smith had arrived. I asked her to have a uniform take him up to interview room three and sat a moment sipping my brew and looking at Dehan across the desk.

"So, we've seen Claire Carter's crime scene, we've reviewed the old case file, and we've spoken to the Reverend James Campbell. Tell me something before we go and talk to our witness. What's your take so far?"

She tilted her paper cup this way and that a few times, studying the thin, black liquid inside.

"What do they say in England? As mad as a box of frogs? This guy is as crazy as a box of Mexican beans with big hats and moustaches dancing the Lambada while hacking at each other with giant machetes."

"Unexpected but undeniably visual. You care to enlarge on that?"

"Yeah, they're all wearing pink tutus too."

"Tutus too?"

"Mm-hm." She sighed. "He is the obvious choice. He has mommy issues and then some, but I have a couple of problems with him. First is that, if I read him right, his big problems kicked in *after* he saw his mother butchered, not before."

I made a "psh, maybe" face and said, "Thin."

"Shut up, you asked. Also, Alvarez said he either had alibis for the other killings, or he couldn't link him to them in any way. And I don't want to walk into the trap of believing it's him just because he's the kind of man who'd do that."

I nodded several times. "Very commendable. And I have to say, overall, I agree. But both the alibis and the timing are weak. Alibis can be fabricated and broken, and just because you can't show he was connected to the other killings, it doesn't mean he wasn't. As to when he went over the edge, we have only his word to go on. You can be as crazy as a Mexican jumping bean and still be as smart as Albert Einstein. His mother might well have bedded one guy too many, he might have come home and found them in bed, the guy goes, and he loses it with his mom. The manner of the killing expresses his deepest frustrations with her and triggers a spate of subsequent murders."

"Might well and may have, Stone. It still boils down to: 'He's the kind of guy who could do this.' That's not evidence."

I offered her a lopsided grin. "Did you ever get her to learn?"

She frowned. "What?"

"Your grandmother, did you ever manage to teach her to suck eggs?"

"That's funny. I must remember that for the next time you lecture me."

"*I?* Lecture *thee?* Never! Come on, let's go see if this guy can bring any light to the affair."

We took our coffee upstairs and collected a third cup on the way to interview room three. Dehan opened the door, and I followed her in. Oliver Smith was in his midthirties, with dark hair that wasn't brown or black and gray eyes that were frank and honest and a little feminine, without being effeminate. He stood as we entered and, as I set down his coffee in front of him, he held out his hand.

"Are you the detectives investigating the murder on Watson Avenue?"

I showed him my badge, and Dehan showed him hers while I said, "I am Detective John Stone; this is my partner, Detective Carmen Dehan. How do you know about that murder, Mr. Smith?"

We all sat while he managed a combined smile and frown.

"Well, it *was* on the news last night, but aside from that, I have . . ." He stared up at the ceiling for a moment, sucking his teeth. "How can I put this . . . I have certain *business* with the Church of the Holy Family, and I went there a couple of times yesterday. That was how I happened to see what I saw, and, later in the day, I happened to notice that there was a lot of police activity. So I made a point of watching the news last night . . ."

He spread his hands and made a "so you see" face. I made an

"oh, I see" face to go with his "so you see" one and glanced briefly at Dehan. She understood and got up to leave the room and check if the murder was on the news, and if so on what channels and at what time. When the door had closed behind her, I smiled at Smith.

"It's good of you to come in. Lots of people prefer not to get involved."

He gave a small snort. "The truth is, Detective Stone, modern society does not encourage social responsibility." He laughed and leaned forward, reaching to lay his fingers on my forearm. "I am not a Republican—*or* a Democrat, for that matter—but I do see a federal government that is ever more overbearing and controlling. And . . ." He shrugged. "The more Big Brother takes responsibility, the less responsibility Joe Public needs to take. There was a time, not so long ago, when Americans felt responsible for each other. You still see it in rural areas, in places where the Christian ethic is still deeply rooted."

I smiled, mildly, and waited. He watched me a moment, returned the smile, and spread his hands.

"I feel I am responsible for the community in which I live and try to do my part."

"You're not a native New Yorker, are you, Mr. Smith."

He laughed out loud. "That is a sad indictment on New Yorkers, Detective Stone. I would not be so harsh. Especially in the last twenty years, New York has turned around. I think New Yorkers have found themselves. Though it is true that, as an urban sprawl, a vastly overpopulated urban sprawl, there is not the kind of cohesion you might find in rural, northern New England."

"Is that where you are from, Mr. Smith?"

"No, I am from Alaska." He chuckled at my expression. "You would expect me to be called Ooa, Nivikanguak, or Aglukak? The most common names in Alaska are Smith and Brown, Detective. The Inuit names are a minority."

"You learn something new every day, if you're paying attention," I said. "So, let me get my bearings here. You were at the church. You say you have some business with them. Do I gather you are a lay brother or something of that sort?"

He shook his head, still smiling, with what I could only describe to myself as a humorous twinkle in his eye. I had the feeling I was talking to the maiden aunt I'd never had.

"No, Detective Stone, I am a journalist. I run a magazine, but that's not important. The truth is, I am not even a Christian. Life has taught me to be an atheist. Believe me, you don't grow up in remote Alaska, watching the seasonal workers come and go, and remain a believer! But that doesn't mean I can't see the worth of Christian values. Not . . . !" He raised his right hand. "Not the values of the Old Testament, but those put forward by Jesus in the New Testament." He shrugged. "So I help by contributing in a fairly substantial way to their good works, and an educational project we are developing. Basic Christian values are good values, whether you are religious or not."

"Forgiveness rather than retribution . . ."

He chuckled. "The thing is, Detective, and this is where Christianity falls down, the Christian values may work for the individual, as a guide through life, but they do not work for society. That poor woman who was murdered, her family and loved ones may, following Christ's teachings, forgive the killer. But, as you suggest, society cannot do that. Society must hunt this killer and bring him to justice, and there must be retribution. If we tried to build society on Christ's teachings, it would fall apart, and chaos and anarchy would reign. That is just one reason why I am an atheist."

I nodded. He watched me a moment and smiled. "Your partner has gone to check if the murder was on the news, and probably to establish at what time and what channels. It was on NBC at half past midnight. Would you like to hear my testimony? I am happy to repeat it for your partner."

I gave a small laugh. "Yes, please."

He took a moment, as though gathering his thoughts, with his hands folded in his lap. "I had been at the church. As I said, I am engaged in setting up a project with Father Cohen, to help children who are the victims of violence . . ." He paused and hesitated. "Direct or *indirect* victims of violence, to come to terms with their experiences through counseling and positive education. I believe quite passionately that projects of that sort could do a lot to bring down levels of violent crime."

"I agree, Mr. Smith. That is a very commendable project. At what time were you there?"

The door opened and Dehan came in. She pulled out the chair and sat beside me. Smith smiled at her and said, "NBC at twelve thirty?"

She glanced at me, and I smiled. "Is that right?"

She nodded. "Yeah."

"Please, continue, Mr. Smith."

He recapped briefly for Dehan and went on.

"So, I arrived at the church at nine a.m. We discussed the details of the project and did a few sums, then we had coffee, and I left at about eleven forty-five . . ."

Dehan sighed and cut across him. "You are very precise about the time, Mr. Smith. Why were you so aware of the time?"

"Well, Detective Dehan, the simple answer is that I wasn't especially aware of the time. I am a busy man, and I stick to a pretty tight schedule, and I like to be punctual. So I always have one eye on my watch." He did an exaggerated nodding thing which included his shoulders and gave a small laugh. "But it is *also* true that, when I realized I had to come and give evidence about what I had seen, I ran through all the details I considered would be relevant in my mind, to make sure I would be accurate."

I glanced at Dehan. She seemed satisfied, so I asked, "So what happened next?"

"I came out of the church, through those big gates, onto Castle Hill Avenue, and turned left into Watson Avenue. I had only gone a few steps when I noticed some movement over on the right, at the door of one of those redbrick houses that are set back from the road. I believe there are two of them, just after the white clapboard one..."

I nodded. "Yeah, at Claire Carter's house."

"What I now know to be Claire Carter's house. The door had been flung open, and a man emerged in a hurry. What struck me was that he did not close the door behind him. He left it open and ran down the steps into the front yard. There he stopped running but walked very quickly across the road and got into a car. It was one of those cars that opens automatically when he grips the handle, but it didn't seem to open fast enough for him, and he practically wrenched the door off its hinges. Then he got in and took off. It wasn't quite burning rubber, but it certainly felt..." He paused to think and finally said, "... *urgent*. It felt urgent."

Dehan drew breath but I spoke quickly. "Was he parked near your car?"

"Yes, as a matter of fact, I was parked behind him—not the next car but the one after that."

"What car do you drive, Mr. Smith?"

He grimaced. "I'm afraid it's a little pretentious. I have a 1969 MG MGB."

I smiled. "Very nice. Right-hand drive?"

"Yes, with the original spoke wheels."

"Superb. What car did this man get into, Mr. Smith?"

"Ah, yes, that was an off-white Ford Kuga. I'm afraid I did not get the plate. He took off toward Castle Hill and then turned left and vanished."

Dehan was making notes and asked, without looking up, "Can you describe him, Mr. Smith?"

"Yes, um... Well, he was sort of nondescript. Five ten, average build, neither overweight nor thin, yet not athletic either. He was wearing jeans and a padded jacket, but not a hoody. It was sage green, and he had medium-length sandy hair. There was no style to his hair, no side parting or anything like that. What you might call a Julius Caesar style. His shirt..." He paused to think again.

"I wouldn't like to say what he was wearing under his jacket. I am not sure."

"Is there anything else," she went on, writing without looking at him, "anything at all that you can tell us about him, what he did, what he looked like, sounded like, smelt like, anything about his car, what it was like inside, decals, badges, decoration, wheels, tires . . ."

She trailed off, and he watched her while she wrote.

"No," he said finally. "There really is nothing else that comes to mind, or that struck me as important at the time. I'm sorry."

"Not at all." I shook my head. "You have been very helpful." I smiled. "Are you a car enthusiast?"

"Well." He was self-deprecating. "I am interested in classic sports cars, from the 1960s."

"On your way out, you might have a look at mine. It's the burgundy Jaguar, Mark II, 1965. I have the original plates framed at home."

His eyebrows shot up. "Oh, now that is a lovely classic. Yes indeed."

I stood. "You said you were a journalist, Mr. Smith?"

He stood too. "Yes, very boring, I'm afraid. Nothing exciting like investigative journalism. Just bog-standard stuff."

I held out my hand, and we shook. "Thank you for coming in, Mr. Smith. We'll let you know if we have any more questions for you. And we may call on you to testify in court, if the man you saw is in fact Claire's killer."

"That's absolutely fine. I am happy to help."

He left, and the door closed behind him. I looked down at Dehan. She finished writing, looked up at me, and shrugged.

"It corroborates what Edna said, and gives us a slightly better description of the killer. Aside from that, it's not dynamite."

I nodded, then shrugged and gave my head a twitch. "Maybe." I glanced at my watch. "Let's go and see Frank, see if he and Joe have anything better for us."

SIX

I pulled onto Bruckner Boulevard, headed east, and said, "So, what do we know?"

She didn't answer but pulled her hair behind her neck and tied it into a knot. The watery sun we'd had earlier had increased to a warm, russet glow which reflected in her shades. But she raised them onto her head now to squint at me.

"We know that Frank will lecture us on the impossibility of establishing an accurate time of death from the condition of the body, but we also know that our main suspect, such as he is, was seen by two separate witnesses leaving the victim's house, in a hurry, at noon. We know he left the door open, as Benny found it four hours later, and that he got into a cream or off-white Ford Kuga."

She went quiet for a while. I turned onto White Plains Road and started accelerating north. She started talking again.

"We also know that he is smart. He knows the cops are going to try and make sense of what he does, and search for patterns and clues to his motivation, so he litters his MO with red herrings to keep cops like Alvarez chasing their own tails."

She stuck out her bottom lip and drummed a brief tattoo on her knees with her palms.

"And we also know that he was active from the first of January, 2014, until the third of January, 2015, and then went off the radar, but has now returned."

"Do we know that?"

She blinked at me and asked, "Don't we?"

"It *could* be a copycat."

"He knows things only the killer could know."

"That's not exactly accurate, Dehan. He knows things that were not released to the press. But he could have acquired that information by working with the cops or the forensics teams, or being involved in some way in the investigation. Or he could know the original killer." I shrugged. "We have to consider the possibility that the original Mommy's Boy stopped killing because he was somehow confined." I shrugged again. "I don't know, either in prison for some other offense, or in hospital, and met somebody inside whom he told that he was the Mommy's Boy killer.

"It is also possible that the killer is simply a friend of his. We should not discount too easily the possibility of a copycat."

"Okay, but it still holds that we know he stopped abruptly on the third of January, five years ago. And that the killings have started again and appear to be identical. So that begs two questions: one, what made him stop? Two, what has caused the killings to start again?"

I turned right onto East Tremont and headed east toward Silver Street.

"Do we know anything else?"

She shook her head. "Anything else at this stage is conjecture, Stone. Before we go any further, we need to talk to Frank and Joe and see what they have for us."

I grunted. "Two gets you twenty they won't have very much. This guy seems to be very aware of forensics, and of the way cops think."

Shortly after that we pulled into the Jacobi and made our way to the ME's department. Frank was in his small, untidy office when we arrived, sitting behind his steel desk, going through forms. He looked up, and I noticed he had shadows under his eyes. I sat opposite him in a chair made of blue synthetic wool and chrome tubing, while Dehan leaned on the doorjamb. Frank shook his head.

"What can I tell you? She bled to death." He rubbed his face with his hands. "She was practically exsanguinated."

He sighed and stood, then walked out into the autopsy room, speaking over his shoulder.

"There is no physical evidence of how he gets them to comply. She was not a small, weak woman. Like all the others, she was on the large side, and by no means weak."

Dehan pushed off the jamb, and we followed Frank over to the body. He pulled back the sheet to reveal the waxy, pale corpse.

"There was no bruising to the jaw or the face, no damage to the knees or the legs. He didn't punch or kick her into submission or unconsciousness."

Dehan gazed at the body. "Drugs?"

"I'm doing the analysis now, but I doubt we'll find anything. I haven't found any puncture marks, and there are very few drugs that work that quickly to paralyze someone, yet leave them conscious enough to know what is happening to them. There is mandrake, as you found out recently, but it takes time to work, and it kills. I really doubt he used any kind of narcotic."

"So he threatened her into submission."

He shrugged. "You're the detectives. I am just saying that there is no sign of a fight or a struggle, and she was not beaten unconscious. In fact, she was not made unconscious in any way. Her facial expression shows that she was fully aware of what was happening to her."

I said, "She removed her clothes beside the bed. They were on the floor in a small pile. So he gained access to the house, persuaded her, either with threats or otherwise, to go upstairs, take off her clothes, and lie on the bed."

Frank nodded. "Her condition is consistent with that. Now, here is what happens next: the first wound is the removal of her left breast. He does that in a single, slicing cut, starting at the lower underside of the breast and cutting up and around. The blade was extremely sharp. There is no hacking or tearing of the flesh or the skin. So this was a very fast, skillful, *practiced* cut, and it had a devastating effect on his victim."

Dehan frowned. "Having a boob removed will do that to a girl."

"Don't be facetious, Carmen. What I am telling you is that she went very rapidly into hypovolemic shock, aggravated by what I could only describe as intolerable emotional distress.

"This would have caused her to convulse on the bed, her pulse and blood pressure would momentarily rise dramatically, but then, with the massive loss of blood, both would have dropped catastrophically, bringing about death very quickly.

"And it is at that moment that he plunges the knife into her womb. The bleeding from that wound is minimal, and *after* that he removes her right breast. There is no bleeding from that wound, though it is also performed with skill, in a single cut."

I said, "So he's using two weapons. The knife, which he stabs into her womb, and another, which he uses to remove the breasts."

He nodded. "Joe is looking at the knife, and he'll tell you about that. But in my opinion that knife is nowhere near sharp enough to produce the cuts that removed her breasts."

I scratched my chin, thinking aloud. "The knife—it's a kitchen knife—it has some kind of symbolic meaning. The way he stabs it into the womb, it's Freudian. I wonder if it's for real or one of his red herrings. It's a bit on the nose, isn't it?"

Dehan twitched her head. "Yeah, but cutting off plump women's breasts is pretty on the nose too, Stone. He does it every time. I think it's for real. Even if *he* thinks it's a red herring, it's for real. This is something he feels the urge to do."

"Yes." I nodded. "Yes, that's probably true."

Frank continued. "As with the others, there is no sexual abuse, and nothing from him in the way of sperm, saliva, blood, or hair."

"How about the makeup?"

He went to the workbench, which ran along the wall from the door to the corner. There he shook a mouse that awoke an iMac, rattled at the keyboard, and a moment later Joe's face appeared on the screen.

"Frank, you missing me already?"

"Not much, I gotta tell you, Joe." They both laughed. "I got John and Carmen here, and we were talking about the knife and the makeup . . ."

"The Carter case?"

"Yeah."

Joe shook his head. "No, there is no way that knife is sharp enough to make those cuts. It's like you said, Frank, he's using a scalpel, maybe even an old-fashioned razor, but my money is on a scalpel."

Dehan crossed her arms. "What about the makeup, Joe?"

"He's using the same L'Oréal products he used before. I've checked them all and they are identical. And this presents you with a new problem . . ." He raised both hands like she was pointing a gun at him. "This is just my opinion, but this is either the same guy or a copycat. Now, if it's a copycat, he has copied the MO down to the smallest detail, and that means two things: he knows the original killer, *and* he is fixated with him. My advice, you really need an FBI profiler on this case."

I said, "That's a good point. I was thinking the same, but for a different reason. The removal of the breasts and the knife in the womb, you couldn't get two more direct attacks on symbolic womanhood. But at the same time, you have the elaborate painting of the face, like he is trying to restore her femininity."

Joe was nodding. "Frank and I both agree on this. The makeup was applied postmortem, to dead skin. So he is done with the killing and the destruction, and now he, as you say, tries to restore her to womanhood by painting her."

I sighed and scratched my head. "It *feels*, almost, like two men working together."

Dehan frowned at me. "One dominant, a leader, the other servile but trying to save the woman . . . ?"

I winced at the sound of it. "Something like that. It sounds improbable, even fantastic, but I can't shake the feeling that we are dealing with two people here."

Frank said, "None of us here is qualified to make that call, Stone. You need the Feds."

"How about prints, Joe?"

"Nada, the knife is clean, her skin is clean. There are a number of prints that occur repeatedly throughout the house, and we're in the process of eliminating them. But the frequency and location suggest regular visitors to her house. There is no trace of the killer."

I sighed. "No real surprises there. It was pretty much what we expected. Thanks, Joe, Frank."

We left and made our way down the stairs to the parking lot in silence. There I called the inspector.

"John."

"Sir, it's looking as though we really need an FBI profiler for the Mommy's Boy case. We need a much better idea of who we are dealing with."

"I'll call them and request somebody. Are we making any progress?"

"It's too soon to say, sir. We've just spoken to the ME and the head of the forensics team, but they were able to tell us very little. One thing is clear, and that is that we are not dealing with a below-average intellect. This guy is smart, he knows about crime scenes, and he enjoys leaving red herrings for investigators to chase after."

"Indeed, fine, well, leave it with me and I'll get on to the bureau."

I hung up and stood looking at Dehan. She was easy to look at. She, for her part, did not look at me. She stared south into the cold wind, then she stared north at the massive hospital complex, and finally she stared up at the low, gray ceiling of cloud.

I sighed again. It was a case that made you sigh. "I know what you're going to say, Dehan, but we have no choice. We have to follow the leads Alvarez followed until we find where he went wrong, or until we unearth something new."

She shook her head at the trees that framed the Van Etten Building.

"It feels like we're dancing to his tune, following his lead, chasing the clues he wants us to chase."

I nodded. "And to some extent that is what we're doing, Dehan. But we have to do it and look a little deeper. We have to ask how he corralled us into doing that? Is there a connection between the suspects and the killer? We have to redo the footwork."

"Yeah," she grunted. "I know. And meantime the clock is ticking. Who d'you want to go and see?" I thought about it, but she didn't give me time to answer. She said, "I want to go see Nelson Vargas. I have a feeling about that SOB."

"Okay, but do me a favor."

I opened the driver's door, and she pulled open the passenger door on the other side. "What?"

"You're going to hate this guy. Just remember that he is, in all probability, guilty of several murders. That doesn't mean he's guilty of this particular series of murders."

She offered me a lopsided grin and an arched eyebrow. We climbed in and slammed the doors.

"Did you ever get her to learn?"

I frowned as I fired up the big old beast. "Who learn what?"

"Your grandmother, did you ever manage to teach her to suck eggs?"

I laughed. "Touché."

Dehan made a couple of calls, and we learned from Vice that

Nelson was working at the Mescal, on Park Avenue, Mott Haven. The Mescal was a bar that doubled as a club for the Chupacabras. It was a known place where you could buy just about any kind of narcotic and fence just about any kind of stolen goods. The Cabras tolerated non-gang members, especially if they were known, but it wasn't the kind of place you'd take your maiden aunt for a glass of sherry.

It was open pretty much all day and all night, but it did most of its trade after midnight. I figured if we went right then, at midday, it would be quiet and we stood a chance of finding Nelson there too.

I turned the key, and the big cat roared, and I pulled out onto Morris Park Avenue. Dehan screwed up her face and scratched her head. "Do we actually have a plan, Stone? What are we going to do? Go in and say, 'Hey, Mr. Vargas, suspected of killing and raping a large number of people, what is your connection with Claire Carter, who was murdered yesterday morning?'"

I showed her an arched eyebrow.

"I gather that is a rhetorical question?"

She shrugged. "Kinda, boss. But what *is* the plan?"

"I have no plan right now, Dehan. I just want to look into his eyes and ask him a few questions, to see how he reacts. We have a number of suspects, and there is a good chance they are all there to give us a false scent. I'm actually more interested in Vargas' connection with our killer than his connection with Claire Carter."

She scowled at the passing shops, like they had annoyed her somehow by being there.

"So you're assuming Vargas is not the guy."

"No, right now I am not assuming anything. But I am open to the possibility that the killer is trying to play us the way he played Alvarez. I'm not sure we realize yet how deep his game was."

She grunted, and after a while she asked me, "So what are you hoping to get from Vargas?"

"I'm going to tell him I think somebody is framing him for

murder, and I want to see how he reacts to that, and who he goes to visit afterwards."

She thought for a while, with her bottom lip stuck out. Eventually she nodded and said, "Yeah, that might work."

SEVEN

We arrived at the Mescal at just after one p.m. It was in an area of the Bronx that was made up of an ugly mix of warehouses and the kind of housing you'd only live in if you had no choice. It was on the corner where East 135th becomes that other Park Avenue. It was surrounded by industrial lots and sported a big, burgundy awning with the name of the club scrawled in gold.

The door was open, and inside it was dim and smelt of stale alcohol and cigarette smoke. Juanes was playing on the sound system, and there was a big guy with tattoos behind the bar, reading the *Fortean Times*. He looked up as we came in, and the dead glaze in his eyes said he'd made us as cops. So I decided not to waste time and showed him my badge.

"Detective Stone, NYPD. This is Detective Dehan. Nelson Vargas here?"

He pulled the corners of his mouth down and shrugged, then turned back to his magazine. I leaned my elbows on the bar. "You ever heard of Claire Carter?"

He made the same face at his magazine and shook his head. I snorted a chuckle.

"Your pal Vargas knew her."

"Yeah?" He didn't look at me. He licked a finger and turned the page. "You talkin' a lot of shit and I don't know nothin', cop. You wastin' your time, and mine."

Dehan reached out, took a fistful of the magazine, screwed it up, and threw it on the floor.

"The man is talking to you, punk." She turned to me and frowned. "That smell like burned cabbage to you, Stone? What does that remind me of?"

I gave the big tattooed guy a sweet smile. "She gets like that sometimes. I tell you, it scares me. I never know what she's going to do next. So about Nelson, he needs to know that somebody is trying to frame him for murder, and I need to know who. I figure he does too. So, you know, he needs to talk to us as much as we need to talk to him. So where is he?"

He jerked his chin at me. "Go fuck yourself." He turned to Dehan. "You too, *puta*!"

She nodded at me. "Definitely cabbage . . . *No!* You know what that smell is, Stone?"

"It's definitely familiar, but I can't place it offhand."

"That, Stone, is the smell of marijuana. I swear it."

"Oh, man! I do believe you're right."

The tattooed gorilla threw up his hands. "Come on, man! There ain't no weed here!"

I made a fair imitation of his expression earlier, pulled the corners of my mouth down and shrugged.

"I sure hope you're right, because that carries time, man, especially if you have priors. Have you got priors?" I turned to Dehan. "Have we got probable cause? Do you think we should search him?"

"Tell you what, Stone, before you do . . ." She labored the heavy innuendo. "I'm going to *go to the car* and check in the *manual* if we have *probable cause*. Okay?"

"*Come on!* You can't do this!"

"Do what? What are you accusing us of? What's your name?"

He spread his hands wide and hunched his shoulders. "Come on, man! I ain't done nothin' . . ."

"What's your name?"

"Jose, man. Jose. My name's Jose. I ain't got no weed back here."

I turned to Dehan. "You know what I have heard, Detective? That very often, in establishments of this sort, where there is marijuana, there is very often cocaine too. So, if you have smelled cannabis, it is entirely possible that we will find cocaine as well. So just as soon as you get back from checking the manual, which we keep in the trunk, I think we should search this gentleman to see if he is in possession of marijuana or coke. Remind me, Detective Dehan, what is the penalty these days for possession of half an ounce of cocaine?"

"With priors?" She smiled at Jose. "Well, with violent priors, Detective Stone, a second-time offender can do anything up to twelve years inside. You think this punk might be a violent offender with priors?"

He closed his eyes and raised both hands, like I was training a gun on him.

"Okay, take it easy. I'll go see if he's in."

"Well I sure hope he is, Jose. 'Cause I would hate to have to call for backup and wind up raiding the place, all on your account. I think that would make your friends and employers very unhappy, don't you?" I turned to Dehan and gave a laugh. "I mean, who knows how much stuff we'll find here!"

"You can't do that, man. We have friends. We got protection."

Dehan leaned on the bar and narrowed her eyes at him. "Really. Well, if you don't go talk to Nelson right now, you're going to need all the damned protection you can get, because you'll not only have us on your ass, you'll have the Cabras on your ass too. Now move, punk!"

He walked away, muttering obscenities in Spanish, and I watched him push through a door at the back of the club that had a plaque reading "Private" on it. I followed, and Dehan came close behind me.

Through the door there was a short passage with a locked door to either side. I thought Vice might be interested to know what was behind those locked doors, but today would not be the day they found out. Instead I moved on to the door at the end of the passage that had a plaque that read "Office" on it. I rapped on the plaque and pushed the door open.

It was like a scene from a dime thriller from the fifties, only the clothes were all wrong.

There was a big, oak desk with a guy behind it smoking a cigar. It smelt like a good Havana. He was staring at me with eyes that were so mad they were crazy. Instead of a double-breasted Italian suit, though, he was wearing a black T-shirt with a death's head on it, and over that a denim jacket with the sleeves torn off.

Leaning on the desk, also staring at me, was Jose. His expression was a weird mix of outrage, terror, and astonishment.

Then there were what Spillane would have called the goons, two of them sitting in easy chairs at a small coffee table that had probably seen more coke than it ever had coffee. They were big, seasoned, stupid, and dressed like their boss, only their bare arms and their faces were covered in intricate, detailed tattoos. The one with his back to me, craning his head around to look, had a mohican, while the other had a long ponytail. They both got to their feet.

I smiled at the guy behind the desk.

"Hello, you must be Mr. Vargas. I am Detective John Stone, of the NYPD, and this is Detective Carmen Dehan." I reached in my jacket and pulled out my badge. "We have four units discreetly parked on Canal Street and East 138th. All I want is to talk to you." I pointed at the guy I guessed was Vargas. "So this need not get ugly."

It was like he didn't speak English. He turned to the two goons, his lip curled with contempt, and he snarled, "*Echenlos. Maten los si hace falta.*"

Dehan is fast. She trains in Krav Maga and Jeet Kune Do and takes it pretty seriously. Vargas was halfway through his instructions to his men when she stepped forward and smashed the heel of her boot into the back of the mohican's head. By the time he slumped forward across the coffee table, she had already vaulted over the back of his chair and, as the ponytail scrambled to his feet, landed a sweet right straight to the tip of his chin. He went down like a sack of wet sand as I cocked my Sig Sauer P226 and had it trained on Vargas' cigar. I spoke quietly.

"You want me to light that for you, Mr. Vargas?"

He slowly raised his hands. Dehan pulled her piece and shoved it in Jose's face. "Go tend bar, Jose." She grinned malevolently. "And if I were you, I'd skip town. I don't think this is going to be a very healthy environment for you from now on."

I put my Sig away, but Dehan kept hers handy, and we both sat at the desk as Jose left on hasty feet and closed the door behind him. I was pretty sure he'd be heading for California and a new identity.

Vargas said, "What do you want?"

"Maria Ortiz ring any bells with you?"

He shrugged and made an ugly face. "Maria, how many fockin' Marias in the world?" He jerked his head at Dehan. "Your fockin' name is probably Maria."

I growled, "Watch your tongue, Vargas. You need to be making friends right about now, not enemies. First of May, 2014, Maria Ortiz called the cops to complain that you had threatened her with rape and murder. Five days later she was murdered."

He looked up at the ceiling and laughed a laugh that said he was bored but amused by our stupidity.

"This again? Yeah, I remember now. Fat bitch." He leered at Dehan. "You know? Sometimes I like a bit of *carne*." He glanced at me to see how I was taking it. "A bit of meat you can get a hold of. I remember she was sexy. She made me crazy always fockin' laughin', always so fockin' happy. That made me wanna make her scream." He laughed. "Bot in a nice way. You ever done that,

Detective Maria? Scream with pleasure? I joss wanted to give her a nice time, a nice party. She was a fockin' whore and I told her, 'Come and have a little party with me and some nice friends! We gonna have some fun!' And the fockin' bitch told me no. She's a fockin' whore and she tells Nelson Vargas no. It made me so mad. I told her, party or no party, I am gonna fockin' own you, and then I'm gonna gut you like a fockin' fish and cut your fockin' arms and legs off."

He grinned at me. "Things you say when you're mad, right? I didn't mean it. I told your boy Alvarez the same thing. People say things when they're mad. Besides, I was with like twenty guys when she was killed. Right here.

"Say, what happened to Alvarez? He was a good boy. I knew him when he was a kid. He made good, right? Up from the streets, became a detective. I haven't seen him around. He skip town?"

I ignored his questions. "So you had an airtight alibi for the time of the killing. The problem with false alibis, Vargas, is that sometimes they turn around and bite you in the ass."

He shrugged. "I wouldn't know."

Dehan cut in, "So how about Claire Carter?"

"Who now?"

"You heard me. You threatened her too. You want to tell us about that?"

He shrugged again and spread his hands, appealing to me as a guy. "You know how it is, dude. Women. It's like streets. You never know them by their names. You know them by the bars, things like that. You tell me, the bitch with the . . ."

I didn't want to hear any more so I cut him short. "She was white, forty-three years old, plump, the way you like them. Lived on Watson Avenue, opposite the church. She had a little club going and you wanted in on the action. She told you no. So you threatened to kill her."

He observed me with hooded eyes for a long moment. Finally he said, "She was killed? I didn't know that. That's what bitches get, see . . ." He turned his eyes on Dehan. ". . . when they give the come-on to a man and then tell him no. She was always laughin', jokin', kind of cute and fun, and then when you get hot and wanna make your move, she tells you you can't. That kind of bitch gonna get hurt. That's the way it is."

Dehan didn't blink. She said, "Jose work here every night?"

He frowned. "Yeah. Why?"

"Was he here all this week?"

"Yeah? You think Jose killed this bitch? He didn't. He was here, man. He didn't even know her."

"Where were you the night before last?"

"Right here, all night, with my boys."

She smiled. "Yeah? Was Jose one of those boys?"

He froze. I chuckled and stood. "Don't get up, Vargas. We'll see ourselves out. Thanks for talking to us."

His goons were starting to stir and groan where they lay. Dehan was still smiling as she stepped past them. She winked at Vargas where he sat staring at us with rage in his eyes. "Good security you have here. Everything's real tight."

I was surprised to see Jose still in the bar. He was standing by the door looking sick. I put my hand on his shoulder and shoved him gently outside toward the Jag.

"Get in. We're going to take a ride."

Dehan got in the back, and Jose climbed in the passenger seat up front. I gunned the engine, and we took off toward the Grand Concourse to join the expressway. As I turned from Park Avenue onto 138th I said, "You're in some trouble, Jose. You need some powerful friends right now. Vargas is one crazy son of a bitch, and he blames you for letting us in."

Dehan spoke up from the back. "You don't realize right now just how serious that is. He is going down for the murder of Maria Ortiz and Claire Carter. And as far as he's concerned, it's your fault that we nailed him. You know from experience, Jose, how that ends. You'll be lucky if he only kills you."

He swallowed, and I could see his hands shaking in his lap.

He'd seen what Vargas did to people who let him down. It was slow, painful, and ugly. I gave the screw another turn.

"You might have saved your skin. I doubt it, but you just might have, if you hadn't got in the car with us and driven away. Now you have no hope."

Dehan spoke from the back again. "Now you have to make some choices. You can make smart choices, or you can make some really bad choices. You can talk to us and the Feds, in which case we will do everything we can to persuade the DA to give you immunity, or you can go back to Vargas and plead for your life."

I took over before he could answer.

"Both outcomes are foregone conclusions. If you can give the DA Vargas and his network, it's a cinch she'll give you immunity in exchange. If you go back to Vargas and plead for your life, it's a slam dunk. He'll tie you to a chair and take his sweet time killing you."

We were on the expressway, headed for the river and Bruckner Boulevard. He was staring out of the windows like a cat on its way to the vet to have its balls removed.

"Where are you taking me?"

"To the Forty-Third Precinct. I'm going to put you in protective custody while you think things over. I'm going to tell Vargas where you are, to help focus your mind. And then, when you've thought things through, you and Detective Dehan and I are going to have a conversation. After that, who knows? If you're lucky I'll hand you over to the Feds and they'll give you a new life."

He sank back in his seat, and we went the rest of the way in silence.

EIGHT

Inspector John Newman, the station chief, was watering his bonsai on his windowsill overlooking Story Avenue when we knocked and went in. He looked carefully over his shoulder and smiled.

"Ah, John, Carmen, come in." He finished watering and said, "Sit down. You have news for me? Are you making progress?"

We sat, and he eased himself into his chair behind the desk.

"Possibly. At the moment we have a couple of witnesses who saw somebody leaving Claire Carter's house at noon. The descriptions agree, but unfortunately they describe him as nondescript. He got into a white Ford Kuga and drove away. It's not a lot to go on, not enough for a BOLO, and forensics has so far given us very little.

"So meantime we're looking at a couple of different angles on the leads Alvarez already had. They are a little more hopeful."

He laid his fingertips along the edge of his desk and nodded at them, like he was comforted they were all still there.

"Such as?"

Dehan answered. "So far we've spoken to James Campbell, Mary Campbell's son. He has a serious issue with women. He believes women are the original sin, created by Satan, and he has built his whole ministry on that premise. His alibi for where he was the night his mother died sounds shaky, and we plan to look into that in more depth, and we need to check his alibis for the times and dates of the other killings."

"That's a lot of work."

I answered. "Yes, sir. We've also been talking to Nelson Vargas. He seems to have risen through the ranks of the Cabras since Alvarez had the case. He now runs the Mescal Club, on Park Avenue, and he had four guys riding shotgun. His alibi for Maria Ortiz's murder and for Claire Carter's is the same. He was at the club with his boys. It's a pretty weak alibi . . ."

He cleared his throat. "It's only weak if you have some compelling evidence to counter it, John."

I nodded. "I agree. We managed to persuade one of his boys to come with us. We have him in protective custody right now and he's considering offering the DA a deal. We would recommend she takes it. He also needs to talk to the Feds about witness protection. Vargas could lead them a long way down the chain to Nogales and Ciudad Juárez, and maybe beyond."

"All right, I'll talk to the DA and to the bureau, but let's stay on task. The fact that Vargas hasn't got rock-solid alibis for those two killings does not of itself mean he is guilty of them. We need real evidence, witnesses, and forensics. What else have you got?"

I grunted. "At the moment it's more a case of what we need than what we've got. We need a couple of guys to work through Campbell and Vargas' alibis and check them out. With Vargas it's going to be pretty much all the same: he was with his boys at the club, but canvassing the victims' neighborhoods might throw up witnesses. It's worth a try.

"Campbell has different kinds of alibis, and each one will have to be checked. If we can have a couple of uniforms to do that, we'd like to go and talk to the last two of Alvarez's suspects, George Allen, who is now living in Rochester, and Golam Heitz."

His eyes rose to meet mine. "Golam Heitz?"

"Yes, sir, he was an orderly at the hospital where Sharon Lipschitz worked."

"Very well. You have learned nothing more from this latest killing?"

"Well, sir, we have learned that the perp seems to know a lot about how the police operate and think. He tries to be a couple of steps ahead. Which leads me to one more request. I think we need an FBI profiler to give us a clearer picture of just who this man is. He seems to be smart, unlike most serial killers. He seems to have issues with his mother. But this is all surmise on my part and Dehan's, and also Joe at the lab and Frank..."

"That is no mean surmise."

"Thank you, sir, but we really need an expert to tell us where this character is coming from."

He made a note in his pad and spoke as he was writing.

"Very well, I'll put in a request. Meantime, set your team to work and see what you can get from this... um..."

"Jose Budia."

"Jose Budia, whom you have in protective custody. Anything else?"

We told him there wasn't and left. On our way down the stairs I asked Dehan, "What the hell did Vargas say that made you kick that guy in the head? You could have killed him."

She didn't answer till we'd reached the bottom. Then she stopped and turned to face me.

"He said, '*Echenlos. Maten los si hace falta.*' That means, 'Kick them out. Kill them if you have to.'"

I nodded. "Good call."

"Thanks."

Ten minutes later O'Brien and Olvera reported to our desk. O'Brien was a redhead with freckles and pretty blue eyes. I dispatched her to find a board where we could stick our photographs and make notes and observations.

Olvera was six foot two of willowy darkness with a hooked nose and dark, humorous eyes. Dehan handed him the file and told him to make four separate lists of the alibis of James Campbell, George Allen, Nelson Vargas, and Golam Heitz. And then systematically set about testing each one of them.

O'Brien returned with the board, markers, and erasers, and we set her to work with Olvera while we put our pictures up with observations and comments. By the time we were done, I was no clearer in my mind than I had been when we started. So I leafed through the file, found George Allen's number, and called him. I was surprised by the answer. It was a woman.

"Mr. Allen's office. How may I help you?"

"This is Detective John Stone of the NYPD. I'd like to speak to Mr. Allen, please."

"May I ask what it's about?"

"You can ask, but I won't tell you."

"Very well, please hold."

I didn't have to hold long. After thirty seconds a deep, gravelly voice said, "This is George Allen."

"Good afternoon, Mr. Allen. This is Detective John Stone of the New York Police Department."

"My secretary already told me that. What do you want?"

"I run a cold-case unit at the Forty-Third Precinct, and we are taking another look at your wife's murder."

"Oh . . ."

"I was wondering if you could spare us half an hour to go over . . ."

"There is nothing I can tell you now that I didn't tell Detective Alvarez back in 2015."

"With all due respect, sir, we have over twenty cold cases under our belts, some of them much more than five years old. And most of them were solved by taking a fresh look at old evidence. It would be very helpful for us if you would let us come and see you in Rochester and ask you a few questions."

His sigh was almost a groan.

"Fine. When do you want to come over?"

"If we leave now we can be there by six thirty this evening, if that's convenient."

"It's not convenient, Detective. It's a damned nuisance. But I guess I'll have to put up with it. It's the big, redbrick house on the corner of Troup Street and South Washington. I have a dinner appointment, so I will expect you to have finished by seven."

"Thank you, Mr. Allen. We'll do our best."

I hung up and sat looking at Dehan a moment, with my mind elsewhere.

"Grab your coat, Dehan. Let's go to Rochester."

It was five and a half hours' drive to Lake Ontario, through some of the most beautiful forest landscapes on Earth. It was no less beautiful in winter than it was in spring, summer, or fall, though at times that beauty was concealed by dense mist or heavy rain.

We hadn't time to collect a bag from home, so we stopped at Kmart on the way and got the essentials. A couple of hours later we were in the Catskills cruising at somewhat above the speed limit in comfortable silence.

It was as we were skirting the lake at Whitney Point that Dehan broke the silence and asked me, "Stone, if you were going to do any other kind of job, what would it be?"

I thought for a moment.

"Well, we had already decided that I would retire to somewhere in New England and, like Dr. Watson, write about how you solved all these cases. I could call it the Dead Cold series, featuring Detective Carmen Dehan, the sexiest, most kick-ass detective in the NYPD. How about you?"

She smiled. "While you're writing my memoirs?"

"Mm-hm."

"I don't know. Maybe I could work at an infants' school or a nursery."

I laughed out loud and was astonished when I glanced at her to see that she looked hurt.

"Oh," I said, without thinking. "You're serious! Okay, here I go, watch me backpedal like a thing possessed."

"You think they'd let me?"

"Why not? I think you'd be wonderful. And, joking aside, the kids would always feel safe."

"Don't, Stone."

"I don't just mean because of your skills, but, you know, you are very capable, cool in a crisis, levelheaded . . ."

"You mean it?"

"Absolutely. Hey! If I feel safe with you in a situation like we saw today, how are two dozen kids going to feel? The girls would all want to be you and the boys would all want to marry you." I did a fair imitation of a four-year-old: "When I gwow up, I wanna mawwy Mrs. Thtone!"

That made her laugh a little more than I expected.

"You don't like this case, do you?"

She shook her head. "No. Those poor women. I try not to think about it, but what they must have gone through, Stone. It's inconceivable."

I glanced at her. Ahead the road coiled darkly among trees into mist.

"You thinking of handing in your badge?"

She didn't answer straightaway. She gazed at the road ahead for almost a minute and finally said, "No . . ."

"Doesn't sound very convincing. If I was interrogating you, I'd think you were lying."

She reached out and put her hand on my knee. "I'm not lying, but I'm not telling the whole truth either. What if I was pregnant, Stone?"

A jolt high up in my chest and a hot burn in my belly made me look at her.

"Are you?"

"I mean, what if I got pregnant? Imagine, a situation like today. Or what this freak does to women with that knife. If I was pregnant . . ."

I waited, glancing at her occasionally. I switched on the fog lights and slowed as we entered a bank of mist, and repeated, "Are you?"

She looked away, at the steep banks that flanked the road, where the dense pines stood shrouded in gray fog.

"That's not really the point."

"It's not?"

She shook her head and after a moment said, "No, not really."

I gave her a minute. Then started to talk quietly.

"I'm feeling a little lost here, Dehan. I want to understand, and I can tell you're feeling distressed. I want to be there for you, but I'm not quite sure what point you're trying to make."

She turned to face me and smiled suddenly. Next minute there was a tear in her eye, and she gave a small, wet laugh.

"Ignore me, I'm just being stupid. I didn't expect the sight of Claire . . ." She bit her lip, swallowed, and took a deep breath. "I didn't expect it to affect me so much. You know, you expect to get sick, throw up, feel queasy. You don't expect the emotional shit. Empathy, pity, compassion . . ."

I frowned. "I would always expect those things from you."

She bit her lip. The tears spilled from her eyes, and she looked away with her hand over her mouth.

"I'm sorry."

"You're okay, Dehan. Sometimes you need to cry, let it out."

She looked at me and nodded, swallowing and sniffing. I pulled a handkerchief from my pocket and handed it to her. She smiled, gave a weak laugh, and blew her nose. I twitched my head and shrugged.

"Of course, it's different with men. We don't need to cry. But, you know, girls need that kind of thing."

She thumped my shoulder and then my knee. "Idiot!" But she was still smiling.

"I don't know what's wrong with me."

I knew it wasn't, but I asked anyway. "Is it that time of the month?"

"You know it's not. You keep better track of it than I do. Besides, I don't get PMS."

"Let me ask you something."

"What?"

"You have faced death in the past."

"That's not a question."

"Bear with me. You have faced death, and you have even had to take a life."

"Yes."

"We have both faced pretty gruesome sights in the past, and it has been stressful and difficult to deal with."

"Yes."

"What is different about this particular murder?"

She took a deep breath. "You and your focused, closed questions."

"What is different, Dehan? I think it's an important question."

"I can't put my finger on it."

"I think you can, but you don't really want to."

"You're being mean."

"Not at all. Shall I say it?"

"What's different about this case is that it is all about mothers."

She studied me for a moment, dabbed her nose, and said, "Explain."

"For a start, all the victims were mothers. Then, you were the one who spotted the fact that every one of them had at least one son. The first suspect we spoke to railed against women and in particular his mother. All of the women are . . ." I hesitated. "'Earth Mother' types. They were all on the plump side, generously built, with large breasts. And of course, the key feature of the murders is the killer's cutting off those breasts. The theme that runs through this gruesome case is the mother."

"You think that's why it's affecting me so much?"

"I think that's part of the reason, Dehan."

She didn't look at me when she asked, "Only part?"

We were climbing now, and the mist was clearing. The tall pines crowding the hillsides stood stark green against a heavy, leaden sky. I waited a moment, then said, "You're questioning your commitment to your job, because this case has made you more aware of your own identity as a woman, and as a potential mother. Maternal instincts are very powerful drives. It's natural that you would not want to put a baby at risk. Especially if it were your own."

"I guess..."

"Nor would you want to put yourself at risk, if you knew you were necessary for your baby's survival."

I turned my head and looked at her. She was staring back at me with moist eyes.

"Dehan," I said. "Are you pregnant?"

She opened her mouth and licked her lips.

"I don't know, Stone," she said, "I don't know."

NINE

It was half past six and already dark by the time we pulled up outside George Allen's house. We climbed out of the Jag and stood looking at the old, gabled, Victorian redbrick standing on the corner. It was narrow and tall against the dark sky, with large bow windows on the ground floor and the floor above.

We climbed the steps to the wooden porch, and I rang the bell.

George Allen was not what I had expected. I am not sure what I had expected, but it wasn't George Allen. On the phone he had sounded aggressively authoritative, like a man used to giving orders and being obeyed. The man who stood at the door was probably in his early sixties, a little stooped, dressed in a gray cardigan with sagging pockets and carpet slippers. A smell of pipe smoke followed him to the door.

But when he looked me in the eye, I could see the same harshness I had detected in his voice. He said:

"Yes?"

"Mr. Allen? George Allen?"

"Yes."

"I am Detective John Stone; this is my partner, Detective Dehan. We spoke on the phone . . ."

"I am aware we spoke on the phone, Detective. Come in."

He stepped back and gestured to his left, toward an open door. Through it we came to a comfortable, old-fashioned drawing room. There was a fire burning in the grate. Leather armchairs and a sofa surrounded it at a comfortable distance, and there was no coffee table to bang your shins on. Instead there were lamp tables and occasional tables set beside the chairs and the sofa. The walls were papered in burgundy stripes, heavy bulls-blood drapes hung over the windows, and the floor was carpeted with large, red Persian rugs over bare boards.

Over on the far left, half the room stood in darkness around a dining table with six chairs, a heavy wooden credenza, and drapes that I imagined concealed French doors onto a backyard.

He followed us in and closed the door behind him.

"I haven't time to offer you coffee or tea. As I said, I have an appointment. I can offer you a drink. Please, sit."

We told him we were fine, and Dehan sat on the sofa. I lowered myself into a leather armchair, and he stood beside the fire. He wasn't going to make us comfortable.

He didn't wait for me to ask him any questions. He went straight in.

"Margaret and I were divorced. She had custody of the children, Alex and Fiona. I should never have agreed, but you do what you think is best. One assumes the children will be better off with their mother, so I agreed to her having custody provided they could visit me on occasional weekends and during vacations.

"We'd been divorced for a year. I was still living in New York, not far from Margaret, in the Shorehaven area. The kids had come to me for the weekend. No doubt she was entertaining one of her gentlemen friends..."

Dehan cut in.

"That's the first we've heard of that, Mr. Allen. Could you clarify that? It's the sort of detail that can be crucial."

He took a deep breath and pulled a pipe from his cardigan

pocket. He turned it over in his fingers for a while, and when he spoke his voice was barely audible.

"This is very painful. The reason Margaret and I broke up was that she had been conducting . . ." He raised his eyes and looked slowly around the room, like he wasn't sure where he'd left the rest of his sentence. "She had been conducting a number of affairs, mainly with men she knew only in passing."

"Mainly . . . ?"

"Entirely with men she knew only in passing."

I scratched my head. "Did you mention this in the original investigation?"

He shook his head. "I'm afraid I didn't, and I have been struggling with it since I spoke to you on the telephone. It isn't only the pain of being betrayed by the person you most trusted and . . ."

He fixed his eyes on his pipe again and Dehan said, "Loved."

"Yes, loved. There is also the humiliation. Bad enough if the affair is conducted with a man ten years younger than yourself. But when it is random men she has met at a playground with the children, or at the supermarket, it is too humiliating to endure. So when people asked me why we were separating, I lied and said we had simply grown apart and Margaret wanted to move on. I grew so accustomed to the lie, I suppose, that when the police asked me about Margaret I told them the same thing. I realized it would be a high-profile case, and I couldn't face her promiscuity being dragged through the national media."

I nodded. "I can understand that, but why the change of heart?"

"I read about the girl on Watson Avenue. It made me realize that if I had been honest from the start, Miss Carter might not have been killed. If Margaret's killer was among the men she picked up, you might have caught him."

Dehan spoke softly. "It's too late for Claire Carter, but it's not too late for his next victim. You need to tell us everything you can remember."

He turned from the fireplace and walked into the dining room. It was an oddly jerky walk, and his slippers scuffed the carpet as he went. He stood at the credenza, and I heard the rattle of glass. When he came back, it was with a generous measure of amber liquid I took to be whiskey. He resumed his position by the fire.

"We were married for twelve years. When I met her she was pretty, shapely, not overweight, graceful, happy, lively, and huge fun. While I was going out with her there were always a dozen other men hanging around in the background, phoning her, texting her late at night. I am not a jealous man, but it began to get on my nerves, and we had a couple of rows about it. She seemed to moderate her behavior..."

Dehan cleared her throat. "Excuse me, Mr. Allen, you said that there were men hanging around her, calling her, and texting her. What was there in her behavior that she needed to moderate?"

He gave an ironic snort that bordered on the scornful.

"Let me ask you something, Detective. I can see from your ring that you're married. Do men call you all the time and send you texts at midnight and one in the morning?"

"Mr. Allen, my personal life..."

"This is an answer to your question, Detective. Do they?"

"No."

"Right, because men, even womanizers, rarely go where they are not invited. You are a very attractive woman, and I imagine that like most attractive people you get your share of men coming on to you. But I am also pretty sure that when that happens, you cut it short and leave the man in question in no doubt about his chances of success. Margaret was not like that. She loved attention, and she loved male attention even more. More than that, she would deliberately put herself in situations where she would attract notice. Everything she did, from going shopping and taking the kids to the park, to going to the gym, invariably ended up with her somehow getting into conversation with one man or another.

"However, after we'd had our rows and I told her I did not think I could live like that, she did moderate her behavior and began to discourage unwelcome attention. Unwelcome for me, not for her."

He sighed and took a pull at his drink.

"But it didn't last. It couldn't last. She was never sincere about changing, because she simply saw nothing wrong with it. To her it was simple, harmless fun. And perhaps there are some men who can see it that way. But I am a very private man, and honestly, I resent intrusion into my family." He gave a dry laugh. "If I had been the one constantly pursued by women and receiving mysterious text messages at one in the morning, I am quite sure it would have been a different matter altogether.

"As it was, what my demand did was to drive her into secret. She started staying longer at the park and the gym. I began to get home from work to find she was not back yet. Then she started leaving the kids with friends and picking them up when she was through with her encounters. Finally she started making excuses for going out at night."

He paused, swirling his drink around in his glass.

"I hired a private detective and had him follow her for a week. In one week she saw four separate men."

Dehan asked, "When you say, 'saw' . . . ?"

"When I say 'saw' I mean had sex with. She saw many more than that, and flirted with them and played games with them. But in that week she had two men visit her here, went to another man's apartment, and went clubbing with a fourth, with whom she stayed the night. That was a Friday, when she told me she was staying with Karen, a friend of hers." He paused again and spoke into his glass. "During this time she had grown plump on self-indulgence."

"Was the club she went to a place she frequented?"

"I believe she went there a few times."

"Can you remember the name of the club?"

He looked mildly surprised. "I should be able to. It was what ended my marriage. It had one of those 'bad boy' names you associate with Mexico, Arizona . . . It's like a drug . . . mescaline? Mescal . . ."

"The Mescal Club, in Mott Haven?"

"Yes, that's the one."

"She frequented it?"

"I wouldn't go that far, but she went more than once."

Dehan glanced at me and leaned forward with her elbows on her knees.

"I know this must be painful, Mr. Allen, and I apologize for having to bring this all back. But, did your private investigator tell you the names of any of the men she met with?"

His voice came bitter and twisted. "The ones she screwed that week, yes, but there were many more the week before, and in subsequent weeks. You would need volumes to hold them all."

"Do you have his report?"

He nodded. "When I made the decision to tell you about her adventures, I imagined you would want to see it. I have it here."

He walked to a small writing desk by the window, opened the flap, and pulled out a manila file, which he brought over and handed to me. I leafed through it quickly. There were typewritten pages and a number of large, glossy photographs.

"Mr. Allen, where were you on Friday, the third of April, 2015? The day your wife was killed."

He raised an eyebrow at me. "Seriously? After all this time, you're going to try and pin it on me?"

I shook my head. "No, not at all. I'd just like to hear the details from you."

He sighed. "As I told the investigating detective at the time, I had taken the children to Broadway to see *Bright Star*, at the Cort Theatre. I collected the tickets at the box office with my credit card, and I paid for dinner afterwards at Carmine's, also with my credit card. Your Detective Alvarez checked all this."

"And how about the day before yesterday, Mr. Allen? Where were you at noon?"

"In a meeting with my boss and six other area sales managers. It lasted from eleven a.m. until one, when we went to lunch. The company is SuperWare. We produce software for supermarkets. The company is based here in Rochester, and I am the regional head of sales. If you are going to check on my alibi, I would be grateful if you would do it discreetly. It's not the kind of thing that does wonders for your reputation. I am three years from retirement, and I'd like to get there with my reputation intact."

I nodded. "Sure, I understand. I think that's all, Mr. Allen. Obviously, if you think of anything, or remember anything, please do let us know. We don't know where or when this killer is going to strike again. Or indeed *if* he is going to strike again. I'll be honest with you. We need all the help we can get."

He shook his head. "I have given you all the help I can give you, Detectives. I was on the periphery of Margaret's life, and we were divorced by the time she died. She was practically a stranger to me by then."

We left him shortly after that. It was cold, and our breath billowed into condensation as we approached the car. I checked my watch. It was approaching seven p.m. Dehan read my thoughts and said, "We'll get home at midnight."

We climbed in the car and slammed the doors. It was as cold and damp inside as it was outside. I pulled my phone from my pocket, did a quick search, and called the Hyatt Regency. I booked a double room and smiled at Dehan.

"The hell with it," I told her. "'Not sure if I am pregnant' is good enough for me."

It was a short drive over the bridge to South Avenue and the Hyatt, on the corner of Main Street. We checked in, showered, and dressed in the same clothes we'd arrived in, and strolled down to the dining room, where we ordered smoked salmon and sirloin steak, with a bottle of sparkling water and two tonic waters while we waited.

When the waitress had gone, Dehan reached across the table and held my hand. She said, "You don't have to do this. You can have a martini, and order some wine . . ."

I shook my head. "Wrong. I do need to do it. We do this together."

"It might be a false alarm. It's just two weeks overdue."

"So we'll do the false alarm together."

She flopped back in her chair and her cheeks colored.

"Did I ever tell you exactly when I fell in love with you?"

"Wow, buy a guy a drink!"

"You didn't even know me. I was a rookie at the station. I walked in and you were balling some guy out for a sloppy investigation, right there in the middle of the detectives' room. I had never been in love. But right then I knew I would never love any other man. Can you believe that?"

I squeezed her hand. "Unfortunately there is no answer I can give to that question that doesn't make me sound like an asshole."

"Some uniform dork came up to me and told me to steer clear of you because you were a royal pain in the ass. He said that, a royal pain in the ass, and did I want to get a drink later. I told him to go to the gym."

I raised an eyebrow. "The gym?"

"That's what he said. I told him he had a better chance of pulling a muscle than he had of ever pulling me." I laughed while she smiled. "See?" she said. "We were made for each other."

TEN

The salmon came, and we ate in silence for a while. Then Dehan surprised me by saying, "George Allen is not the guy."

I glanced at her and returned to my salmon. "I have to agree."

"So, that leaves, of Alvarez's suspects, Campbell and Vargas, and of course Golam Heitz, who we haven't spoken to yet. I'm guessing you noticed in the file Allen gave us..."

I nodded. "I did. She went several times to the Mescal. Vargas wasn't running it back then, but he frequented it, like all the Cabras. The private eye didn't mention him by name, but I'm pretty sure he's in the pictures with her at the door, leaving. We can get the lab to enhance them."

She gave her head a small shake as she pressed a cracker and salmon into her mouth. "Be cam, bu' dash him."

"We can but that's him?"

She nodded. "Mm-hm."

"So that connects Vargas with three of the victims: Claire Carter, Margaret Allen, and Maria Ortiz. But we have no connection with Olga Hernandez, Sharon Lipschitz, or Mary Campbell."

She wagged her knife at me across the table.

"You said something yesterday which struck me as important."

"Keep this up and you're going to make me blush."

"Yeah, right. You said that it felt like there were two people at work in these killings. One who painted her and tried to redeem her, and another who brutally destroyed her. What if, and I am shooting the breeze here, but what if there actually were two killers?"

I shrugged my eyebrows. "It's not unheard of, but we need more than my feelings to go on . . ."

"Yeah, sure, but what if one of those killers was a man whose whole purpose in life was to redeem, and save souls? What if that man had a congregation? And what if the other killer shared something crucial with this redeemer: a deep, violent, misogynistic streak? What if they both hated women, but where one wanted to destroy them, the other wanted to save their souls?"

I leaned back in my chair, chewing my lip.

"That is a very compelling idea, Dehan. We haven't a shred of evidence, but it is a powerful idea."

She laid another piece of salmon on a cracker and eyed me a moment.

"It goes further. If both of them were at work, that duality would give them the objectivity to plan the murders in such a way as to leave red herrings and misleading patterns to confuse the cops."

"They would be able to talk to each other and plan, and get as much of a kick out of confusing the cops as they did out of killing the women."

"Exactly. And if those women were connected in some way with the congregation, they would not hesitate to open the door to a preacher."

I nodded for a bit, looking at the angles.

"But let's not get ahead of ourselves. We have a couple of problems here. The first is, how many women do you think Campbell attracts to his church? My money is on not many. And following from that, we have no indication whatever that Olga Hernandez and Sharon Lipschitz were ever anywhere near Campbell's church."

"True." She stuffed the last piece of salmon in her mouth and chewed, watching me across the table. "But," she said, and swallowed, "we should explore the relationship between Vargas and Campbell to see if there is one, and we should also try to find out if those women were ever at his church. Let's face it, Stone, all six women are linked somehow to Mommy's Boy. If we find what links those women, we must find the killer, or killers."

"That link might be the church, or the axis of the church and the Mescal Club. A truly unholy alliance."

"Punishing women they deem to be whores."

My phone rang, and I pulled it from my pocket. It was the chief. I tried to catch Dehan's eye, but she was gazing at the black glass of the dining-room windows, pierced by small lights from beyond.

"Sir."

"John, where are you?"

"In Rochester, sir. We've been talking to George Allen."

"Why, the man had a watertight alibi . . ."

A stab of irritation made me interrupt him.

"He also had information he had never given to Alvarez. Information which might have an important impact on the case."

There was a moment's silence, then he said, "I see, well, good. Good. When will you be back?"

I was about to tell him nine in the morning, thinking we could rise at four. But watching Dehan across the table I said, "Lunchtime. It's a five-and-a-half-hour drive."

"I see. Fine, fine . . . Jose has agreed to talk to us. But he says he'll only talk to you and Carmen. Try and get back as soon as you can. Good work, John. As always."

I hung up.

"Jose has agreed to talk."

"That's good news."

The waitress came and took away our plates. Another brought us our steaks and told us to enjoy them. We ate in silence for a while, until I laid down my knife and fork and said:

"You want to come off this case?"

"No." She said it, then shook her head.

"At least until we know for sure, one way or another." She studied me across the table while she chewed. I went on. "You could work from the station, looking at the alibis. If I need backup, I could take Olvera. We should keep you out of harm's way."

"No."

We ate a little more in silence, and she said, "Joe is going to tell us something about Vargas. It will either incriminate him in our investigation, or it will provide us with information we have to hand over to the Feds. Either way I want to be a part of that. And I want to know if Campbell is involved. If he's not, I want to know who is. I can't do that sitting at a desk, Stone. It will drive me crazy."

"You know a lot of stress and trauma can affect the baby, even in the first few weeks."

Her face softened into a smile.

"Stone, don't get your hopes up. I'm just a couple of weeks overdue. I may not be pregnant at all."

"The baby could be born with a hideous birthmark."

"Shut up!" She laughed.

I smiled. "Okay, but tomorrow you phone to make an appointment with Dr. Kelly. If the test is positive, we have to keep you out of harm's way. Agreed?"

She nodded. "Agreed."

———

WE ARRIVED BACK in the Bronx at half past noon and went straight to the 43rd. We briefed the chief on what Allen had told us. He said he'd spoken to the DA and to the Feds and they were willing to cut a deal with Jose. So we spent half an hour inspecting the file Allen had given us from his private eye, and had Jose brought up from the holding cells.

When we went in to talk to him, he looked nervous and drawn, like he hadn't done much sleeping in the last twenty-four hours. I sat at the table opposite him, and Dehan leaned against the wall with her hands in her pockets.

I said, "So, what have you got for us, Jose?"

"I'll give you Vargas and Vargas' boss. I can tell you where they get their H, their blow, their weed, and their pot. I can tell you who supplies them and who distributes for them. And I can tell you where and how it comes across the border. I can name names, man. I can tell you who Vargas has killed and who he's had killed, and who his *sicarios* are. Him and his boss. But you gotta give me immunity. I need a guarantee from the DA, and I need to get on the witness relocation program, man, because my life won't be worth shit."

Dehan snorted. "It's not worth that now, smartass. It stopped being worth that the day you joined the Cabras."

"Hey! Don't give me a hard time, man. I'm cooperating here. If you ain't gonna give me immunity, what the hell am I doing here?"

I leaned back in my chair and gave him the dead eye.

"Relax, Jose. You have your immunity. But the information has to be enough to bring Vargas down with his organization. Is it that good?"

"I can tell you everything."

"I'm guessing you don't want to use your attorney."

"Juan Mendez? You gotta be kidding me." He shook his head. "The Chupacabras own that guy. He does everything for them, from concealing evidence to money laundering. Nah, you need to appoint me a lawyer, man."

I nodded and glanced at Dehan. She said, "I'll tell the chief to call the DA and get a counselor."

"But hold off on the Feds."

She left the room. I opened the file Allen had given me and pulled out the photographs taken outside the Mescal Club and laid them out in front of him. He frowned.

"What?"

"Recognize any of these people?"

His eyes took in my face with quick, darting movements.

"What are you trying to do? Is this a trap or something?"

"No, Jose. You have your immunity. Your lawyer is on his way, and the interview is being recorded. I just want you to tell me if you recognize any of the people in these pictures."

He hesitated. "Yeah, that's Nelson." He looked a little closer. "Juanito, Leandro . . ."

"Okay, but that is Nelson Vargas?" I pointed at him in the picture.

"Yeah, man. That's him."

"How about this?" I pointed at Margaret Allen. "Who's she?"

He stared at the picture awhile, then frowned a bit.

"Yeah, I recognize her. But that was three, four years ago, maybe more. She came to the club a few times. Nelson liked her. She was different, you know? Not like the chicks that usually hang out at the club. She had more class."

"What happened?"

He shrugged. "Nothing happened. She stopped coming to the club. That's it. Why have you got photographs of her?"

"He ever sleep with her?"

"I guess, yeah."

"She ever turn him down? How come they stopped seeing each other?"

He spread his hands and shook his head. "I don't know, man. She just stopped showing up. That's all I know. What's the big deal?"

"Is Nelson religious?"

"We don't usually talk about that shit, you know? Most of us are Catholics, and we all know we're going to hell. So we don't talk about it."

"Has he ever talked about religion? You ever heard him?"

The door opened, and Dehan came in. He watched her sit down, and I repeated the question.

"Has he ever talked about religion in front of you? Have you ever heard him talk about his religious beliefs?"

"Yeah, okay, yeah he has. He says he's a Satanist. But I think that's just like a pose."

"Has he ever mentioned women in the context of religion?"

"Women? Like the Virgin Mary?"

Dehan said, "Or Eve, Mary Magdalene . . . The question is a simple one, Jose. Has he ever talked about his opinion of women in relation to religion?"

He thought about it for a while. Eventually he pulled down the corners of his mouth and shrugged.

"I guess. He says, like, that women are inferior, weaker, more stupid, with no integrity. He uses that word. He likes that word. He reckons women are like an inferior species."

Dehan took a deep breath and sighed heavily. "Does he go to church?"

"What's the big deal with religion and women? I thought you wanted him for . . ."

I snapped, "Just answer the question, Jose."

"I never seen him go to church, but that don't mean he don't go. Most Sundays I go to church with my mom and my sister. So I don't know what he does. He don't go to the same church as me, anyhow." He screwed up his face. "But it's not a big deal. You know what I'm sayin'. Guys in the Cabras got all the chicks they want. We don't talk a lot about women. Or religion."

I slipped a piece of paper across the table to him. On it I had written the names of the six victims.

"You ever hear him talk about these women?"

He ran his eyes over the list.

"Maria, Maria Ortiz. He liked her. She was like a whore, but not a street whore. You know what I mean? She had like regular guys who would go see her. She was nice. I wanted to see her, but she had a rule, no Cabras. She had a place on East 151st, South Bronx, over the Huaxciaxtla eatery."

Dehan asked him, "So how'd he take it when she told him no?"

He laughed. "You don't say no to Nelson, know what I'm sayin'. You say no to Nelson he gonna cut you. He's a crazy son of a bitch. I seen him cut a guy's face off for tellin' him he don't wanna do something."

"So what did he do?"

"He told her he was gonna go over there and do some bad shit to her."

"And did he do it? Did he make good?"

He looked down at the table and shook his head. "I don't know. I know she was killed after that, but I dunno if it was Nelson who done it. Usually, when he iced someone, he would talk about it. It was prestige for him. That made him higher in his standin', you know what I'm sayin'? It was like he had more respect, the more people he killed. But he never said nothin' about killing Maria."

I pointed to Claire Carter's name. "How about her?"

"He was talkin' about some white bitch he wanted to screw. He said she was a whore, had some kind of club. Nelson likes fat women, and he said she was fat. Like Maria. Maria was fat too. He's always sayin' how a man needs a big woman. Some shit like that."

"So what happened with this white woman?"

"I dunno, man. He jus' stopped talkin' about her."

I pointed to the rest of the names. "None of these others mean anything to you?"

"Maybe Olga Hernandez. But that's a pretty common name. Might not be the same one." He frowned. "Wait a minute . . . Olga died too. Wait, these are the girls. I remember now. These are the girls who was killed by that freak."

I held his eye. "I want you to think very carefully, Jose. Did Olga Hernandez have any contact with Nelson?"

His jaw dropped and he flopped back in his chair. "Oh, man! Oh, holy shit, dude. You cannot be serious! *Nelson?*"

I gave him a moment. His eyes searched the ceiling. He shrugged.

"Man, she was in the hood. She was Colombian, real sweet, you know? Colombian chicks got a special thing. She lived over a mission or a chapel or some shit on 149th and Courtlandt. I don't know if he knew her. She had a kid. She was big too, real fun, party chick. She wasn't with the Cabras, but she was around. Know what I'm sayin'?"

Dehan asked, "You never saw them together or heard him talk about her?"

"No, man. I can't believe you're trying to pin, what was his name? Them murders, that was five years ago, man. You tryin' to pin that on Nelson?"

"I have one more question for you, Jose. Do the names James Campbell and Mary Campbell mean anything to you?"

He blinked a lot and looked around the room, at the walls and the ceiling.

"Campbell? Jim Campbell? That the preacher?"

Dehan said, "Yeah, how do you know about him?"

"Yeah, Nelson gone and seen him a couple of times. Not to his service, but private. He gets deep sometimes, and he sometimes says that a warrior needs a spiritual path, especially when he gets older. Like the samurai, know what I'm sayin'? When you do a lot of killing and cruel shit in your life, you need a spiritual path to balance that. I get what he's talkin' about. I can see that."

"So you're telling us that Nelson sought out Campbell as some kind of spiritual guide, or guru?"

"He never talked about it. But I know he went to see him a few times. Me, I prefer Zen, and Tao, and that shit."

There was a knock on the door, and a uniform leaned in.

"Chief says the assistant DA is here, Detectives."

I gave him the nod, and he went away. I turned back to Jose and slipped a piece of paper across the table to him with a pen.

"I want the name and the date of every woman Nelson ever killed."

"Every woman. You don't care about the dudes?"

"The Feds will ask you all about that, and they are the people who are going to save your skin. But before I hand you over to them, I want to know about every woman Vargas ever killed, or threatened to kill."

He shrugged. "Well, that's easy, man. You already named her. That was Maria Ortiz. Apart from her I don't know no more bitches he might have killed. You ask me about rape, bitches he give a slapping to, then I'm gonna need more paper, know what I'm sayin'? But kill? Nelson killed dudes, dudes who stood in his way, dudes who wanted trouble with him. Those dudes he wasted. But women . . ." He shrugged again.

I sighed, and after a moment we went to see the chief and the ADA.

ELEVEN

ADA Ron Bushy was tall and lean with a trim goatee and hair that was a bit too long for an assistant DA, but you wouldn't want to tell him so. He was leaning against the windowsill with his arms crossed and his left eyebrow in what looked like a permanent arch.

Inspector John Newman, the chief, was behind his desk with a face that didn't know whether to be pleased or worried. Dehan was on the black leather sofa, and I was leaning with my back against the door, listening to Bushy.

"I think I need to have things clarified a little. What exactly are we investigating here? And who exactly is investigating it? Are we looking at gangs and organized crime, are we looking at cross-border smuggling, are we looking at murder or a serial killer?" I drew breath to answer, but he went on. "And who is doing the investigating? Is this a cold case that you are handling, Detective Stone, or is it a current case? Is this federal jurisdiction? In which case, why are they not investigating it?"

Dehan stared at the ceiling and spoke in a loud, startling voice.

"I blame the government," she said. "The government should lay down guidelines for criminals, so they know exactly within what parameters they are allowed to commit crimes. Any crime committed outside the permitted parameters will be considered . . . a crime . . ."

ADA Ron Bushy was not amused, but I was, and I snorted to show my appreciation. Before he could say anything, I spoke.

"We are investigating a cold case that went hot a couple of days ago when Claire Carter was murdered using the MO of the Mommy's Boy killer, five years back. So far it's a serial killer, murder, within the jurisdiction of the NYPD, Forty-Third Precinct. With me so far, ADA Bushy?" He didn't answer, so I went on. "One of the suspects in that investigation, one Nelson Vargas, is a high-ranking member of the Chupacabras, a gang in the South Bronx. During our investigation into his connection with the Claire Carter murder, we came across a witness who is willing to talk to the Feds about the Chupacabras operation, and in particular Nelson Vargas, in exchange for immunity from the DA and being put in the Witness Relocation Program."

"So whose witness is this? Yours or the Feds'?"

Dehan groaned softly. I pretended not to notice. "We've spoken to him, and we think he's given us everything we can use in the Mommy's Boy investigation. So we're ready to hand him over to the Feds. He figures he can give them Vargas, Vargas' boss, and the whole network down to Nogales and El Paso. Maybe beyond. I think it's true."

"Based on what?"

Dehan answered for me. "Based on over forty years' experience between us. Based on having talked to the guy and listened to him instead of getting our panties in a twist over these damned crooks not observing the rules of procedure in the committing of crimes. Based, ADA Bushy, on being damned good cops and doing our jobs."

She left a ringing silence when she stopped. I stepped into it and said, "You have a different opinion, ADA Bushy? Based on what?"

He raised both hands. "Okay, you made your point. Inspector, what's your view?"

The inspector knitted his brows at his desk. "If I had not agreed with Detectives Stone and Dehan, I would not have wasted the district attorney's time. Believe me, you will not find two better investigators—*anywhere!*"

Dehan stood. "Speaking of wasting time, we have an investigation that is already five years old. Are we going to offer Jose immunity, or are we just shooting the breeze here?"

Bushy scowled. "You need to moderate your tone, Detective Dehan."

"Yeah? Eat my shorts, Counselor. How's that for moderation? You want moderate tones, leave your attitude at the door. This is the Bronx, we eat white-collar punks for breakfast. You want to throw your scrawny weight around at the Forty-Third, you come to the next Mommy's Boy crime scene. After you've thrown up your Earl Grey and French croissants, then you tell me to moderate my goddamn tone, and ask me what I base my goddamned opinions on!"

I watched her say all this with undisguised admiration. When she had finished, ADA Bushy looked at the chief for support. The chief cleared his throat, but Dehan spoke first.

"Are we done here, sir? We have leads to follow up, Jose needs his immunity, and we need to contact the Feds to come and take him away."

He wouldn't meet her eye but nodded and said quietly, "Indeed, Carmen. I suggest you inform your suspect that the ADA is here with the papers. John will join you in a moment."

"Thank you, sir."

She left and didn't quite slam the door. I watched Bushy gearing up to open his mouth and stopped him. "She's the mild one. Get me going and I throw grown men out the window. You ever been to a crime scene where a sadistic serial killer has been at work? She saw her first just a couple of days ago. It gets to you. I've known it to kick the cocky bullshit out of a few Ivy League assholes. Now, let me ask you a question, Bushy. Did the DA tell you that immunity for our informant was at your discretion?"

"No."

"Then can we cut the crap and get it wrapped up and done? Like Detective Dehan said, we have work to do."

The inspector aimed a frown at me and said, "Indeed, I am sure we all have."

We wrapped things up with Jose, ADA Bushy left, and the chief called the bureau to have them send a couple of agents to collect Jose. Then I tramped downstairs, by way of the coffee-like-substance machine, and found Dehan sitting at her desk with her boots propped on the corner. I gave her a paper cup of coffee-like substance and sat in my chair.

"The Feds are sending over a couple of guys to collect Jose. You get any more out of him? I think we got all he had for us."

"I asked him when Vargas went to see Campbell. He said he thought the visits started maybe four or five years ago. He couldn't be precise. But as far as he's concerned, he may still visit him from time to time. It's something Vargas doesn't talk about much."

I sighed, picked up a pencil, tapped the eraser a few times on the desk, and examined it. I didn't find any answers there.

"We need times, dates . . . We need to know what they spoke about. What they speak about. We need video and audio. We need a judge to sign off on a warrant to tap their phones, and we need a team to follow Vargas."

Dehan nodded for a bit. "Maybe we can liaise with the Feds. They can do all that real easy. A judge is going to buy Vargas the drug dealer-slash-importer a lot easier than he's going to buy Vargas the serial killer. All we've got is a theory and a tiny bit of circumstantial evidence."

I did a little dance with my head.

"We can connect five of the six victims with Vargas. And we can link Vargas with Campbell as a man seeking a spiritual path."

"You don't have to sell it to me, Stone. I already bought it. But it's going to be a hard sell to a judge."

"There's something missing."

"Yeah, evidence."

I chuckled. "Yeah, maybe that's it. So, we need to go talk to Golam Heitz, and we need to go lean on Reverend James Campbell. We also need to talk to . . ." I reached over for the file and leafed through it. ". . . Saul Lipschitz. See if we can find some connection between Sharon and Vargas, or Campbell."

Through the door I saw ADA Ron Bushy leave and reached for the internal phone to call the chief.

"Ah, John, look, I can't condone the way you and Carmen spoke to the assistant DA . . ."

"No, sir, we were out of order."

"Well, that's very big of you. I was going to say that I did enjoy it. However, what can I do for you?"

"We need you to authorize a tail, sir. We think there may be a connection between James Campbell, Mary Campbell's son, who preaches a radical form of misogyny, and Nelson Vargas, whom we know threatened two of the victims with rape and murder, and whom we can connect with five of the six victims. We know that Vargas went, and possibly still goes, to Campbell for spiritual guidance. We need to put a tail on Vargas, and if we can prove they meet more or less regularly, we need to apply for a warrant to listen in on their conversations."

"All right, you can have your tail. O'Connor and Brightman have experience in the field. They're on late tonight. I'll have them report to you. As to the tap, send me what you've got, but from what you've told me, we don't have enough yet for a judge to sign off on that one."

"Thanks, Chief."

I hung up and sat looking at Dehan, who was staring at me. "You called the doctor yet?" She shook her head. "Do it now."

She pulled out her phone and sat looking at it. I stood and went to look for Maria. She was at the front desk talking to a man who wanted to report the abduction of his next-door neighbor by aliens. She was nice to him and asked him to wait.

"What do you want, handsome?"

"I need you to get Mike O'Connor and John Brightman for me. When do they come on?"

She looked at her watch. "It's six, they should be in in a couple of hours. You want me to call them?"

"Yeah."

"Which one? They're not married, you know."

"Really? I thought they'd finally tied the knot. Get Mike for me. He's the butch one, right?"

She sighed and shook her head. "You can't talk like that anymore, Stone." She started dialing. "They'll have you doing gender fluidity awareness classes if you're not careful."

"It's too late for me, Maria. I'm a dinosaur. I'm already extinct."

"More's the pity. Mike, Maria, hey, gorgeous. Yeah, I got sourpuss Stone here wants to talk to you." She was quiet for a moment, giggled, and said, "No, he really is here, and he really does want to talk to you. Yeah, I know."

She handed me the phone and winked at me.

"Mike, Stone."

"Hi, Stone. How's it hangin'?"

"Yeah, good. Listen, I just got through talking to the chief. I need some surveillance done. He said you and Brightman were the guys for the job."

"Yeah, I just heard. Whatcha got?"

I told him about Vargas and Campbell. He said, "Holy shit. What's the timetable?"

"I think the most likely hours are eleven a.m. till two a.m., I can't see anything happening before or after that time."

"Me neither, but that's fifteen hours, pal."

"Yeah, that's why there are two of you. Start tonight, soon as you can."

He grunted, and I hung up and scowled at Maria. "So I'm handsome, but he's gorgeous."

She shrugged. "What can I say. He's Irish. The Irish have that special something."

"Yeah, it's called Guinness."

I made my way back to Dehan. She was still sitting staring at the phone.

"Did you call?"

She shook her head. I reached out my hand, and she gave me the phone. I pressed call. After a couple of rings a woman's voice said, "Dr. Kelly Surgery, can I help you?"

"Good afternoon. This is John Stone. My wife thinks she might be pregnant. She'd like to make an appointment to see the doctor and have a test."

"Oh hello, Mr. Stone. Carmen, isn't it? I have a cancellation tomorrow at nine a.m."

"That will be fine." I looked at Dehan. "Tomorrow at nine then. Thank you." I hung up and handed her the phone. "I'll come with you and hold your hand."

"Thanks." She turned the phone around in her fingers for a while, then slipped it into her jacket. "You want us to go? Let's go talk to Campbell. Ask him about his connection with Vargas."

I nodded. "And then home."

"Okay."

By the time we got to the Church of the Holy Father and Son at the End of Days, dusk was closing in under a heavy gray sky, but a warm light glowed in the lobby and washed the sidewalk through the plate glass doors. We pushed in and saw the doors to the chapel open also, and a powerful, bombastic voice berated the world from within. We crossed the polished wooden floor and stood on the portal of madness, watching the dark mass that was going down inside. I glanced at Dehan and smiled. She had achieved the apparently impossible task of staring wide-eyed while squinting. And I could see why. At least two-thirds of the congregation were women. And James Campbell was not giving them an easy ride.

By their reaction, it didn't look like what they wanted was an easy ride. He was striding up and down the stage, gesticulating violently, pointing a large finger here, there, at all the women who sat gazing at him, weeping, occasionally wailing and clenching their hands in prayer.

". . . Our Father who art in Heaven. I think, I *think*, that's what it says! Am I wrong? Is there a woman out there who can set me right? Does it, in fact, say our *mother* who art in Heaven? Whose name is it, after all, that must be hallowed? Is it our mother in Heaven?

"No! No! And a thousand times *no!*"

I reached in my pocket and switched on the recording app on my cell. He plowed on.

"Was it, I ask each and every one of you vile sinners, was it the *daughter* of God who came down to save *man*kind? No! And, is it *woman*kind that he came to save? No! And do you know why?"

He strode up and down in silence while among his faithful the women fell on their knees, beating their breasts and crying out, "*Save me!*"

"*Save our souls!*"

"*Forgiveness! Forgive us, Father!*"

"*Oh! We are sinful!*"

Then he bellowed, "*I asked you a question!*"

One black woman wailed above the others, "*We are not worthy!*"

His face contorted and the veins stood out in his neck.

"*Because woman is the spawn of the Devil! Because woman was created by Satan to lure Man away from the Father's righteous path! Because it was woman who enticed Man from the path of righteousness to eat the forbidden fruit of the Tree of Knowledge. And I ask you this . . . !*"

He paused, glaring out at the rapt, transfixed members of his congregation.

"I, the Reverend James Campbell, spokesman of God, I ask you this! Answer me, if you will, this question: If Eve was the creation of our Lord the Father, *why* would she disobey our Lord and entice Adam away from righteousness? *Why* would she heed the word of the serpent? *Why* did the serpent not go directly to

Adam? Why, I repeat, *why* would Eve *obey* the serpent Satan if she was indeed the creation of Our Lord the Father?"

His voice dropped to a rasp: "*Well, I shall tell you! She would not! She did these evil things because she was the creation of Satan!*" Another pause, and then, "It was Satan who took the rib from Yahveh's perfect creation, thus rendering him imperfect. It was Satan, the Fallen One, who molded Eve's form from base clay, and it was he who created this faithless, flawed, perfidious, *shameless* creature. And in so doing..."

He took a few paces, blaming the world with his face.

"... in so doing, created *sex*! And with sex did he create Man's great weakness, Man's hunger, Man's lust, Man's hubris in his need to see himself immortalized, not through the Father, but through his own lasciviously obtained offspring! Through this *disgusting* act of copulation does he seek, beguiled by evil woman, to emulate the divine act of creation!

"*Shame!* I say to you, a thousand times shameful, ye, who crawling in the mire are born of the serpent, and seek to drag divine Man down with you!"

There were now several women prostrate, lying facedown on the floor, weeping. One woman on her knees was crying out, "Father! Holy Father! Lead us to redemption! Help us!"

He stretched out his arm, pointing the finger of damnation at them where they lay.

"*Are you ashamed?*"

"*Yes! Yes!*" came the cry from the congregation.

"*Are you ashamed of who you are? Are you shamed that you are the whores of creation?*"

"Yes! Yes! Shame is ours! Father, redeem us! Lead us to righteousness! Lead us to salvation!"

"You? You ask me for redemption? You dare to ask me for redemption when it is you who have brought Man low? You dare to come here to me, begging for forgiveness and salvation, when it is you who have brought mankind to the brink of damnation?"

Now they were all weeping and beating their chests. Some

were beating their own faces with their open hands and tearing at their hair. The men were moaning, rocking back and forth and from side to side, while the women cried out, "*We are not worthy! We are not worthy!*"

"*Then dig deep!*" he thundered. "*Dig deep into your pockets! Dig deep among your ill-gotten gains! Dig deep among the wages of whoring, and pay! Pay for your eternal sin! Pay to spread the word of the Holy Father! Pay! Pay! Pay!*"

And as he railed against them and swore at them and insulted them, they wept and reached into their purses and paid. The money flowed, from those women's hard-pressed, hard-taxed wages, and into the silver bowls that Campbell's two cherubic page boys carried very slowly around the room. I did a rough estimate and figured he pulled in five grand in about ten minutes.

They sang a couple of songs about how no man born of God would ever be damned, but about how women might be saved if they sought the grace of the Father, then they all tidied their ragged clothes and filed out into the dark, ten bucks lighter and easier of soul, just like nothing had happened, and they hadn't been sprawling on the floor, weeping and wailing, fifteen minutes earlier.

As they filed out, Reverend James Campbell watched us from the pulpit, and when the last of his disciples had left the hall he boomed, "I have nothing to say to you!"

Dehan gave a single, dry bark of a laugh.

"The day you have nothing to say, Campbell, they'll be selling Ben and Jerry's in hell."

"Blasphemy!"

"Bullshit! Cut the crap, Jim. You can tell it here or you can tell it down at the station. You choose!"

"How dare you . . . ?"

I started down the aisle and spoke quietly, so he had to listen.

"We dare. Now let's move on. Where do you want to do this: in the comfort of your own madhouse, or in the discomfort of the station house?" He drew breath, and I added, "Do I need to call for backup? We can have two cars flashing lights outside your church in two minutes. You tell me."

His hackles seemed to settle.

"What do you want?"

Dehan answered. "How about we start with you climbing down from the pulpit and we talk on the level?"

He gazed at her a moment with toxic eyes, then came down the five steps and stood staring at me.

"Very well, I am down here, on your level. Now what?"

"You know a man named Nelson Vargas?"

He took a long time answering, but he didn't remove his eyes from mine. Finally he said, "Yes, I know Nelson Vargas."

TWELVE

He moved over to the pews and sat. It was a heavy movement, like the movement of a man carrying a heavy load.

"I have known Nelson Vargas for many years."

I leaned against his stage and watched him a moment, trying to read his body language.

"How?" I said at last. "How did you come to know him?"

"His family were originally from Clason Point, from Randall Avenue. I was raised at six thirty-five Rosedale. We went to the same school. We were never friends. He was mixed up with the gangs from the word go. My drive was always to move away from evil and corruption. The Grace came to me early, and I was already preaching when I was eleven, twelve years old. It got my nose broken, it even got my arm broken once, but apparently it left an impression on Nelson.

"When I left school he was already a member of the Chupacabras, and I sought the path of ministry, and I was guided by the Father to find the true meaning hidden in the holy Scriptures. But eventually, he came to hear about my words, my teachings, and he felt drawn."

Dehan said, "How drawn?"

He blinked slowly, looked away, and then turned to me.

"Ask her not to speak."

I glanced at her, then repeated, "How drawn?"

"Do you mean, to what degree, or in what way?"

"Both."

He sighed. "He came to see me in December of 2014. He was deeply troubled. He had been released from prison just a couple of weeks previously on a charge of possession. He had done a year, or thereabout. I don't recall exactly.

"He had gone home to his mother, and no sooner had he arrived than she began to attack him and rail against him, and *nag* him, as only women know how. He already carried with him a deep-rooted rage at all the injustice he had endured since he was a boy, and he snapped and beat his mother senseless, punching her and kicking her to the ground.

"When his rage had passed, being a Catholic, he felt deep remorse and, above all, guilt at what he had done and called an ambulance. His brothers in his gang were able to alibi him and several of them said they had seen her fall down the stairs. She herself, when she regained consciousness, realized what was best for her and said that she had fallen.

"The thing was, he felt lost and needed a path, a spiritual path, upon which he could make sense of his own rage and his actions in life, and I was able to give him that guidance."

I glanced at Dehan, wondering if she was going to be able to keep her cool. She gave me a small nod, and I asked him, "Exactly what kind of guidance did you give him?"

"I led him to a better, clearer understanding of the function of women in our world, and the true relationship that exists between divine Man, and women, who are essentially evil."

I nodded. "So you allowed him to rationalize and justify the fact that he had beaten his mother half to death."

"That is no doubt how you see it. I saw it as a deeply repressed need to strike out against the evil forces that are dragging mankind to the very brink of hell. I made him understand this, and it brought him a deep peace. In exchange, he helped fund my ministry."

Dehan gave a loud bark of laughter.

"You mean you're laundering his proceeds from drug trafficking!"

His gaze didn't waver from mine.

"Is that a formal accusation? Do you intend to arrest me on that charge?"

I shook my head. "No, but I am interested in my partner's observation. If we were to examine your books, would we find that Nelson Vargas receives any kind of revenue from this church?"

His eyes became hooded. There was something dangerous about them.

"Why don't you get a court order and find out?"

I nodded. "Maybe we will. Let's see how it goes. That isn't our primary interest right now. What I would like to know is, how often do you and Vargas meet? Do you meet on a regular basis?"

His gaze traveled past me to the stage, and his eyes seemed to become glazed.

"Not regular. I suppose he might come around once or perhaps twice a month, depending on how he is feeling. Spiritual clarity is something most people need to renew from time to time."

"And where do you meet?"

"That is an absurd question. What possible difference can it make . . ."

"Here? In the church? What form do your meetings take? Are they prayer meetings? You get down on your knees and pray? Or is it like a counseling session with a therapist? You sit there and he talks and you listen? Or you talk and he listens?"

He took a deep breath and closed his eyes.

"As with all my congregation, it depends on their needs at the time. Sometimes they need to talk, and the Father gives me the grace to listen and give them understanding. At other times they need guidance, so I speak to them, and the Father gives me grace to guide them to the righteous path. And on those occasions we will go to my study upstairs. But at other times what they need is to make an act of faith, and then we come here and we kneel and we pray together, so that the Father will touch them and show them the light."

I smiled on the right side of my face and grunted. "Only it isn't as with all of your congregation, is it, Reverend Campbell. Because Nelson Vargas is not one of your congregation. He does not come here to pray. He does not come here to hear you talk during service. Nelson Vargas comes here to discuss other things with you, doesn't he?"

His lip curled, and there was deep disgust in his eyes.

"I have no idea what you are talking about, Detective. But what I do know is that you are fishing, and if you had a shred of evidence to substantiate whatever it is you are insinuating, I would not be sitting here comfortably in my church, I would be confined in some squalid interrogation room. And pretty much the same goes for Nelson. I don't know what you're trying to pin on him, but clearly you have nothing but your sick fantasies to support you."

Dehan screwed up her face and scratched her head.

"Does he share your hatred of women?"

The contempt was such on his face that his mouth twisted and spittle spilled from his lower lip.

"I told you to keep her *silent*!"

I smiled, and Dehan asked him, "Why don't you ask your Holy Father to silence me, Reverend."

The action was slow, like a slow-motion camera: first his eyes traveled to his left, to look at Dehan under hooded lids, and then his head turned to follow.

"You should be very careful, Detective Dehan. The Holy Father does not care to be mocked."

She didn't flinch. "Is that a threat, Reverend? Are you threatening me?"

"No, woman . . ." He said it like you might say "skunk," or "slime." "I am offering you guidance."

I said, "You didn't answer the question. Does he share your hatred of women?"

His eyes shifted from me to Dehan and back again.

"Let me be very clear about something, Detective. I do not hate women. I simply see them for what they are: the servants of Satan. So, no, he does not share my hatred of women, because I have no hatred of women to share.

"Now, do you ask me, does he share my vision of women? Yes, he does."

I nodded just once. "Yeah, I kind of thought he might. I'm almost done here, Reverend. I just have a couple more questions for you. Do you know a Sharon Lipschitz? Has she ever been a part of your congregation?"

I watched him carefully, reading his reactions, looking for the smallest contraction of his pupils, or the shifting of his gaze. All he did was frown.

"A Jewess. It's unlikely, isn't it, Detective?"

"Yeah, well, you're pretty unlikely yourself, Reverend. And what I saw here this evening was pretty unlikely too. You didn't answer my question."

"I have no recollection of any Sharon Lipschitz, or any Jews for that matter."

"You anti-Semitic, Reverend? You have something against the Jews?"

"You refer to the people who betrayed and condemned the son of the Holy Father?"

I gave a small laugh. "So a Jewish woman would not be your idea of a perfect date, I'm guessing."

"Was that your other question? Because I would like you to leave now."

"No, Reverend, my other question was, what car do you drive?"

"That is no secret. I have a modest Ford SUV. Why?"

"What color?"

He shrugged. "Cream, perhaps white. Are you going to tell me why?"

"Just routine questions, Reverend, like, where were you, the day before yesterday, between ten and noon?"

He hesitated. Then he hesitated some more.

"I was right here, in my church."

"Can anybody corroborate that?"

"Why would they need to?"

"Is that a 'no'?"

"As far as I recall I was alone. I was in contemplation and prayer, but I would have to check if anyone saw me."

Dehan chuckled noisily. "If you are going to fabricate an alibi, Reverend, make sure it's watertight. There is only one thing more incriminating than being caught with a false alibi, and that's being caught in the act."

He scowled at her. "I have no intention of fabricating . . ."

I looked at Dehan and cut him short.

"I think I've seen and heard about all I need and all I can stomach. Have you anything else, Detective Dehan?"

She shook her head. "This Jewish woman has had a bellyful. Let's go."

We made to leave, and he stood. His movements were stiff, wooden. His face expressionless, but taut with repressed emotion.

"They bring a darkness with them, you know, Detective Stone. They cloud your mind and your heart. Where women walk, pain and suffering are close behind. They will hurt you. They will steal your soul, suck out joy and freedom and make you a slave. You should get rid of this one. She is a vampire, sucking out your life."

I stopped to look back at him. There was something almost pathetic in his expression, but it was a pathos that was laced with viciousness and danger. I decided it wasn't worth answering, and we stepped out into the cold night.

We reached the car, and Dehan leaned her ass on the driver's door.

"He's the guy," she said. "It's like I said, Stone. It's why you had the feeling there were two people at work. But Campbell is not the redeemer, he's the brutal predator, the real killer. And Vargas is the freak trying to find forgiveness from his mother."

"As ADA Ron Bushy might say, based on what?"

She pointed past me, back at the church, and an icy breeze made her shudder.

"He has a cream Ford SUV. That guy is out of his mind. He is so full of hatred for women . . ." She sighed suddenly and dropped her arm. "Okay, that's not evidence, but Stone, you know as well as I do that it's them, the two of them. You said so yourself."

"What we know is irrelevant, Dehan. You know that. What it comes down to in the end is what the jury knows—or believes. And right now any decent attorney would have this case thrown out of court before the jury even got a chance to look at it. What we might just get is a tap."

I pulled my cell from my pocket and showed it to her.

"You recorded the interview?"

"Yeah. I think we need to take it to a judge with feminist leanings."

She smiled. "I think that too."

"If we get some positive results from the surveillance, this recording might just swing it. Can we get in the car now? It's cold."

She chewed her lip for a minute, then walked around to the passenger side. We climbed in and shut out the night, but it was still cold in the cab. I fired up the car, and we rolled away.

"Sharon Lipschitz is a loose end," I said after a while. "We need to tie her in. And I want to get a look at this Heitz character. There's something in the back of my mind that's nagging at me and I can't figure what it is."

She was silent for a while, with the opaque lights of the city washing over her as we moved north toward Lafayette. Then she said, "I do."

"You do? What is it?"

"Usually by this stage of the investigation you're all smug because you've figured something out and you won't let me in on it. And this time I'm keeping pace with you and you feel all weirded out about it."

I snorted. "That must be it."

We drove in silence for a little longer, until I turned west onto Lafayette and said, "So, what are we saying happened here? Vargas got out of jail, went home, beat up his mother, and put her in the hospital..."

Dehan took over. "And, being basically a Catholic, he felt profound guilt about what he had done. When Catholics feel guilt, they look for a priest to absolve them. But obviously he could not go to a Catholic priest, because one of the very worst things you can do, according to the Catholic faith, is attack your mother. Mothers are sacred. So he found his way, through the grapevine, to James Campbell, who had recently had a similar experience."

I nodded. "He had either found his mother murdered, or he had murdered her himself... But, for our theory to work, James Campbell must have killed his mother, because otherwise we get into the nightmarish possibility that Campbell and Vargas are copying the MO of whoever killed Campbell's mother. And that is too much."

"So," Dehan went on, "we are saying that Campbell had recently killed his mother when Vargas came to him..." She trailed off. "Unless, Stone, Vargas came to Campbell and told him what he had done, and that inspired Campbell to kill his own mother. Vargas gave him strength, and he in turn inspired Vargas. And *that* was what set them off on the killing spree."

I nodded. "It's horribly believable, Dehan." I turned north onto Soundview. "So, if this theory is correct, what made them stop? And what made them start again with Claire Carter? All we have so far is that Vargas wanted to sleep with her and she said no. And we have no explanation for the long period of abstinence."

There was something else troubling me too, but we were arriving at Story Avenue, where I wanted to drop the recording with the chief before taking Dehan home. So I thought that what was troubling me could keep.

We parked in the lot outside the main entrance, and I went to get out. Dehan didn't move.

"You coming?"

She looked at me like she was surprised I was there.

"You won't be long, right?"

My face told her the question was surprising, but I shook my head.

"I'll wait here. I need to think."

I nodded. "Sure."

THIRTEEN

It was cold, but she was sitting with her ass against the hood of the Jag, trailing condensation from her nose and mouth. Every breath was a ghost released, drifting into the Bronx night to trail over the amber streetlamps and the dangerous parks.

My feet crunched on the frosted blacktop, and she looked up. "Okay?"

"He's going to call Judge Petersen in the morning."

She smiled. "She'd have them castrated at dawn and hung before breakfast if the law allowed."

I returned the smile. "And if it didn't, if she could get away with it. According to the *New York Times*, she's the Republicans' favorite Democrat, and the Democrats' favorite Republican. You ready to go home?"

She shook her head and searched my eyes for a moment.

"No. Let's go to the St. Barnabas, see if Heitz still works there, and maybe they have his address." She shook her head and, in apparent contradiction, said, "You're right. We're developing this theory and ignoring Sharon Lipschitz, who so far doesn't fit in any way. She has no apparent connection with Vargas or with Campbell."

I shrugged with my eyebrows and my shoulders simultaneously and admitted, "Yeah, that's been troubling me. They didn't even live in the Bronx. Her husband, Dr. Saul Lipschitz, is a heart surgeon. His family is rich, but he's rich in his own right. West Seventy-Fourth Street, in Manhattan."

"We've been neglecting Sharon. We should take the long way home and swing by the hospital."

It wasn't that much of a long way home. We took the Bronx River Parkway as far as the zoo and turned left onto East Fordham Road. A minute after that we turned into Lorillard Place and Third Avenue. By the time we got there it was almost nine. The chances of finding Heitz there—assuming he was still employed by the hospital—were slim. But falling prey to a virus or choking on a fish bone are no respecters of nine-to-five, so there was always the chance we'd get lucky.

We rolled through the big gate and left the car in the multistory parking lot, then walked over to the reception. The place was quiet, and the girl at the desk smiled as we approached.

"Help you?"

I showed her my badge. "I'm Detective Stone, this is my partner, Detective Dehan, NYPD, we need to talk to somebody about Golam Heitz. He is, or was . . ."

"Gogo? Oh, sure! He's been here for years. You can talk to personnel, you can talk to the head janitor, or you can talk to Gogo . . ." She trailed off as her brain caught up with her enthusiasm. "He's not in trouble, is he? He's a bit simple, but he ain't bad . . ."

I smiled the way I imagined her favorite uncle smiled. "No, not at all, we just need to ask him a few questions. Were you about to say he's here?"

"Yes . . ."

"Could you call him for us, please? And have you a room where we could talk to him privately?"

"Sure, you just go down that corridor . . ." She stood and leaned across the desk to point. "You're gonna find, on your right, a consulting room. Nobody's gonna use that tonight. You can wait for him in there."

We found the room, which had no windows, a melamine desk, and three blue chairs made of chrome tubing. There was also a blue sofa with a coffee table bearing magazines ranging from *National Geographic* to *Hello!*

Dehan dropped into one of the blue chairs, and I rested my backside against the desk and crossed my arms. Five minutes later the door opened, and a man who was in his late twenties, but somehow had the look and the air of a sixteen-year-old, stepped into the room and stood holding the door open.

I smiled at him, not like his favorite uncle, but like someone who meant him no harm.

"Are you Golam Heitz?"

"Yes, am I in trouble?"

"Not with me. Come on in, sit down. We just want to ask you a few questions. That okay?"

He let the door swing closed and sat on the sofa with his hands laid flat on his lap and his knees pressed together. He looked me straight in the eye and said, "I don't know what the questions are. So I don't know if it's okay. Who are you?"

Dehan pulled out her badge, and I showed him mine. She said, "I'm Detective Carmen Dehan. This is Detective John Stone. We're police officers with the Forty-Third Precinct of the New York Police Department. Our specialty, as cops, is that we investigate old cases that didn't get solved the first time."

He listened very carefully, watching her lips and then her eyes by turns. When she'd finished, he asked her, "Have I committed a crime?"

She smiled at him. It was nicer than my smile. "I don't know," she said. "But all we want is to ask you some questions about something that happened about five years ago. Is that okay?"

"I don't know what the questions are."

Dehan went on. "The questions are about Sharon Lipschitz."

"She's dead."

She nodded. "Yeah, we know that. Did you like her?"

"Is that one of the questions?"

"Yeah."

"I don't mind that question."

"So, did you like her? Were you friends?"

"Yeah, I liked her a lot. When you're slow in the head, people can be real mean sometimes. Especially doctors. They can be real bad, and shout at you and sometimes hit you and kick you, when nobody's looking. But Sharon was never like that. Sharon was the sweetest person in the world. She said we were friends."

"She must have been a very special person for you."

"I just said that."

He said it without malice and without sarcasm, as a simple matter of fact. I asked him, "How long did you know her, Golam?"

"Three years, two months, six weeks, and four days. Do you want to know the hours and the minutes too?"

"No, that's not necessary. Did she remind you of your mother, or an older sister?"

"No. I don't know my mother, and I don't know if I have any sisters."

"Oh, how come? Who gave you your name?"

"My mother saw as soon as I was born that I was going to be a problem, so she left me at an orphanage. The director said I was Jewish and called me Golam Heitz, because he said that was a good name for a Jew boy."

I shook my head. "Never call yourself a Jew boy, Golam. You're a Jewish man, and that is something to be proud of. So, what about the other people at the orphanage, Golam? Was there anyone nice there? Or were they all like the director?"

"There was no one especially nice. I don't like people. I don't like being touched. So I just stayed away until I was old enough to leave. Then I came and worked here."

Dehan gave a small laugh. "I know how you feel."

"Do you?"

"Yeah, kind of. So how come you were able to get a job straightaway here at the hospital, Golam?"

"Because I was at the Zoo Orphanage, on East 191st Street. And that's only one thousand and seventy-nine yards away, or point six of a mile. The founder of the orphanage was Dr. Hoffman, who was a pediatric consultant at St. Barnabas. And he appointed his illegitimate son as director of the orphanage. That was Mr. Garcia. He used to joke that Dr. Hoffman had put a bastard in charge of all the other little bastards."

I scowled. "Boy! This Mr. Garcia seems to have had one hell of a sense of humor!"

"No. I don't think he was funny."

"So he arranged for Hoffman to get you a job?"

"The hospital gives lots of jobs to kids from the orphanage. Usually as janitors or cleaners. That's why they gave me a job."

Dehan leaned forward, with her elbows on her knees. "Golam, did you ever meet Sharon's husband?"

"He works here. I've seen him, and Sharon spoke to him when she was with me. But he never spoke to me. Sharon said he was too grand to speak to anyone below an attending physician unless they were a patient or his wife."

"Nice, so did Sharon introduce you to any of her friends?"

"No. I already told you. I don't like people. I liked Sharon. But I don't like anybody else. Not even you."

She made a sad face, which I thought might have been genuine.

"That's okay, Golam. You don't need to like me."

"Thank you."

"So did you ever see Sharon outside the hospital?"

"Sometimes when she went to her car."

Dehan laughed. Golam looked at her like he knew people laughed sometimes but didn't get why. Dehan said, "No, I didn't mean that. I meant did you ever meet with her when you weren't at work? Did you ever visit her at home, or did she visit you at home, or did you ever meet somewhere that wasn't at work?"

"No."

I said, "You don't visit many people, do you, Golam."

"I told you I don't like people. Why would I visit people if I don't like them?"

"That's a very logical question. I need to ask you a different kind of question now. You have a great memory, right?"

"I remember things how they were."

"So, I'd like to know where you were and what you were doing the day before yesterday, between eleven in the morning and one in the afternoon. Can you tell me that?"

"Yes. I was at home. I slept until twelve. I got up and washed and dressed before I made the bed, because it was cold. Then I had my breakfast and started to prepare things for work. I left home at twelve forty, so at one o'clock I was walking through the door and into the hospital."

"That's extremely accurate."

"That's what happened. I can't be absolutely accurate because that would involve trillions of bits of information and it would take so long to communicate it that by the time I finished telling you, you would be dead, rotted away and decomposed."

"We don't need that kind of accuracy, thank you, Golam. Is there anybody who can confirm at what time you got up, or that you walked from your home, what, twenty minutes away?"

"That's two questions. My home is twenty-two minutes from the reception desk, depending what part of my house you are in. But I don't know if anybody can confirm it. I suppose there must be lots of people who saw me, but most of them probably don't know who I am, and didn't notice me."

"Right . . ." I glanced at Dehan. She gave a minute shrug. I turned back to Golam. "Where do you live?"

"I have the basement apartment at 424 187th Street."

At that moment the door opened and there was a man in a white coat, with a ginger beard and balding ginger hair, frowning down at us.

"What's going on?" He turned to Golam. "Who told you you could leave your job?"

Golam stared at him. "It's the police," he said simply.

"I know who it is, Golam. Go back to your work." To us he said, "What do you want?"

I didn't answer straightaway. I held his eye a moment and asked, "Who are you?"

"Excuse me? You come into my hospital unannounced and start interrogating my personnel..."

Dehan stood and stepped up close to him. "Who are you? We want to know who just stopped us from interviewing a witness. Who are you? If you'd prefer, we can take you across to the Forty-Third and ask you there for a few hours."

His face flushed pink to the roots of his hair.

"Who the hell are you?"

Dehan snarled, "Do you answer questions as well as you bluster? I'm Detective Dehan of the NYPD, and I'm going to ask you again, who the hell are you, and why the hell did you chance off our witness?"

He narrowed his eyes at her, and the flush subsided a little.

"I am Dr. Hoffman, the chief operating officer of this hospital. Now perhaps you will tell me what you were doing interviewing a member of my staff without notifying me."

I pushed myself off the desk and said, "Maybe we will. But then again, maybe we won't. Because we don't need your permission to interview members of your staff, Dr. Hoffman. We do need your permission to interview you, unless we arrest you or take you in as a material witness. How well do you know Golam Heitz?"

His mouth worked, but no sound came out. Before he could answer, I asked him another question.

"How about Sharon Lipschitz? Did you know her?"

He said something that sounded like, "Bababa..." and then, "Of course I did!"

"Of course you did. How well did you know her?"

"I *beg your pardon*!"

"You own the orphanage where Golam grew up?"

"I am one of the trustees . . . the main trustee . . ."

"Has he been diagnosed?"

"What are you talking about?"

"He's autistic."

"Yes, yes, he's been diagnosed. Look, what is this about? Sharon?"

"Yes."

"But you can't possibly think Golam had anything to do with it. He was investigated years ago, and the detective cleared him of any . . ."

Dehan cut across him. "Nobody cleared anybody in that investigation. It went cold, and we're looking at it again. Why were you so keen he shouldn't talk to us?"

He shook his head. "That's not it at all. He is vulnerable." He glanced at me. "You saw yourself that he is autistic. You, the police, can be very aggressive in your questioning, and he can become very distressed. His thinking is very literal, and metaphors, sarcasm, irony, things of that sort can send him into a hysterical fit."

Dehan frowned. "Metaphors can make him hysterical?"

He did a passable imitation of a tough cop from a black-and-white movie. "'Drop the act and quit winding me up, wiseass!' You have three metaphors in there: the act, the winding up, and wiseass. Golam would be incapable of processing that sentence. And he would be even more incapable of understanding it as an answer to whatever he had said. He would become acutely distressed."

I nodded. "Okay, thanks. Now I'd like to ask you again, how well did you know Sharon Lipschitz?"

He shrugged. "I knew her as a colleague whom I had worked with for a number of years. We were not close friends, much less lovers, if that is what you're getting at."

"I'm not. I need to know a few details about her private life, her religious views, how she socialized..."

He pulled down the corners of his mouth and shrugged again. "I can tell you she was a practicing and devout Jew. The subject came up from time to time, regarding various Jewish festivals. Of course her husband was and is a close colleague of mine, and we are friends as well. I would suggest you talk to him, but he's not here, and I know he is trying hard, even today, to forget what happened to Sharon."

Dehan said, "So if I told you that she was taking an interest in a Christian cult that was deeply misogynistic and preached that women were the original sin..."

He didn't let her finish. He burst out laughing so hard his face and head flushed bright red again. Every now and then he would stop and stare at her wide-eyed and start laughing again.

Finally I said, "Okay, Dr. Hoffman, the laughter is getting a bit tedious. How about you answer the question?"

He gave a scornful snort. "I thought I just had."

Dehan snarled, "Try using words."

"Sharon was an intelligent, well-educated woman from a cultured, upper-middle-class family, and she was married to a highly educated, erudite eminence in the field of cardiology. Any such cult or sect would have struck her not only as laughable, but also as deeply offensive. She could have been an eminent doctor. She certainly had the skills, the intelligence, and the dedication. But she married a great man and chose to care for her home and her children. They always took precedence. Her maternal instinct was a powerful, luminous thing, and she displayed it with Golam as much as she did with every patient she cared for."

I said, bluntly, "You loved her."

He didn't flinch. "Of course I did. Everybody who knew Sharon loved her. What happened to her was devastating to all of us. But the notion that Golam might have had anything to do with it is patently absurd."

"What makes you say that? We have officers looking into his alibi right now, but as I understand, it wasn't exactly airtight."

He gave a bark of laughter. "What kind of alibi do you expect from an autistic man who spends all his time alone? But it is his very character as an autistic young man that makes it practically impossible for him to have committed those crimes."

"You're referring to the physical contact?"

"Of course! What else? Murdering somebody is the most intimate contact one person can have with another. Sex merely comes a close second. But the act of physically taking somebody's life . . ." He shook his head. "I don't refer to shooting somebody with a gun or a bow and arrow, or cutting their brake cables. No. I am talking about holding somebody in your arms, pressing your body against theirs, and taking their life, physically, with your own two hands. *That* is the deepest intimacy that two people can have. Nothing could be more intimate than that. So I ask you, how could a boy who recoils hysterically at the mere touch of a hand possibly hold down a struggling woman, remove her breast, and then stab her in the womb?"

Dehan was watching me, chewing her lip. I said, "I don't suppose he could."

Unexpectedly he crossed to the sofa and sat.

"Her murder has troubled me for years. I don't mind telling you that I was in love with Sharon. I told Saul as soon as he introduced me to her. I said, 'You're a good friend, so I have to tell you from the start. I am in love with your wife.' He laughed. He knew I was telling the truth, but he's a big man, inside, in his heart and his soul. And he knew he could trust her implicitly. And me, for that matter. I'll talk to him for you. I'll tell him to contact you. If you approach him directly, he'll tell you to go to hell and wrap you up in lawyers. He wants to forget. But if I talk to him, he might just see you. Now tell me something: I read that there had been another killing. Is there any chance you will find the bastard who killed her?"

I watched him carefully for a few seconds, then nodded. "Of

course. We are very good at what we do, Dr. Hoffman, and somewhere along the line he made a mistake. We'll find it, and we'll find him. By the way, what car do you drive?"

He laughed again, but with a little less contempt. "Am I a suspect now? I drive a BMW i8."

Dehan smiled. "Anyone who describes murder the way you do, Doctor, has to be a suspect. Where were you the day before yesterday, from ten a.m. till one p.m.?"

"Right here, chairing a meeting from ten till twelve, and then interviewing the next generation of great doctors for the hospital. No, I could not have killed Sharon. The reason I spoke like that is because, after her death, I spent many sleepless nights imagining what she went through during those last minutes of her life. It is inconceivable. Hell, Detective, is not a place we go to. It is right here. It is a state we inhabit when people like that bastard enter our lives."

I sighed. "You may be right, Dr. Hoffman. The mind is its own place, and can make a heaven of hell, and a hell of heaven. Thanks for talking to us. And I'd appreciate your help in contacting Dr. Lipschitz."

I pulled a card from my wallet and gave it to him. "Tell him he can call me at any time, day or night. We need to know what connects her with all the other victims, and with the killer."

He looked at the card and put it in his pocket. "Of course," he said. "I am sure he'll be in touch."

FOURTEEN

The next morning we spent an hour at the surgery. The doctor took the opportunity to give Dehan a general checkup and ordered a full screening of her blood. While Dehan was dressing, Dr. Kelly came out to talk to me. She had red hair, freckles, and blue eyes that searched my face from behind a professional smile.

"Haven't seen much of you lately, John."

I returned the smile. "My grandmother used to say that there is no rest for the wicked. She forgot to tell me there is no rest for those who pursue them either."

"How about when they take on the responsibility of a family?"

"What are you telling me, Kate?"

"We have to wait for the results, but some of the signs are there, and then there's the old feminine intuition." She gave a small laugh. "If she isn't now, she will be soon. Are you looking for it, or was this an accident?"

I thought about the question for a moment and gave a small shrug. "Neither. I guess we're not looking for it, but we're not trying real hard to avoid it either."

"You're not a young man, John. Having a child is a hell of a responsibility. And an only child is demanding in a very special way. There is a lot to think about here."

"Yeah." I nodded. "But I didn't want to do too much thinking until we had something concrete to think about."

She gave a feminine little grunt, narrowed her eyes, and smiled all at the same time. It was an expression that said she thought I had it all what the Brits call "arse about tit." The wrong way around.

"Carmen is not young, not in gynecological terms, but she could certainly consider having another child, if she is pregnant. That would give the baby a brother or a sister, which some people consider to be a good idea . . ."

I laughed. "We haven't even got one yet!"

She nodded awhile, blinking at me. "That's kind of the point I'm making, John. You're both cops. You're both accustomed to analyzing situations, exploring angles, planning ahead. But always in the context of other people's lives."

"That's true."

"Now you're going to have to adapt, and apply all of those skills to yourselves and your children, as a family." She gave a small laugh. "Only now you won't be bringing anyone to justice. You'll just be making them safe and happy."

"Kate, I am sure you're right . . ." I gave a small frown. "But I am still not sure what you're getting at. What's your point?"

"I'm just wondering how easy, or difficult, it's going to be to do that if you're both employed as cops. It's not only that the risk to each of you personally is also a risk to the baby, but also the long, unpredictable hours, and the stress you're both under." She hesitated. "Carmen mentioned, in confidence, the case you're working on." She put her hand on my arm. "I'm just saying, it's stuff that needs to be thought about. It's not like you're young parents."

"Sure."

On cue Dehan stepped out of the consulting room. Her eyes were bright, and she was smiling.

"Couple of days?"

The doctor smiled. "It shouldn't take more than that. I'll call you."

I didn't get much chance to think about what she'd said. By the time we got back to the car my cell was ringing. Dehan leaned on the roof of the car while I answered.

"Stone."

"Stone, it's Mike O'Connor."

"You got something?"

"No, I just felt like bonding. Yeah, I got something."

"Okay, so you're a wiseass, congratulations. What have you got?"

"Last night, eleven forty-five, Vargas leaves his club, gets in a Porsche Boxster, and drives to Castle Hill and Homer. There he parked outside the Church of the Holy Father and Son at the End of Days and went inside. He was in there for a little over half an hour and came out again. He got back in his car and drove back to the Mescal, where he left his car and went back inside."

I was quiet for a minute, thinking. "Any other contact?"

"No, that was it. It didn't seem urgent enough to wake you from your beauty sleep."

"Okay, stay with him. Keep me posted." I hung up and leaned on the car opposite Dehan. "Vargas paid a visit to Campbell last night at a quarter to twelve. They were together for just over half an hour, and Vargas went back to the Mescal Club."

She snorted. "So he got a sudden need for spiritual guidance at eleven forty-five, and Campbell is so good he put him on the straight and narrow again after just thirty-five minutes."

"So if he didn't go to see him for spiritual guidance, and we agree he didn't, what did he go for?"

"At midnight? Something that only required thirty-five minutes . . . ?"

"Correct me if I'm making unwarranted assumptions . . ."

I waited. She nodded and gestured at me with both hands. "Sure, go ahead."

"Thirty-five minutes at that time of night is going to be one of three things: a fleeting sexual encounter, a rapid exchange of information, a rapid exchange of some other, physical object. Can you think of anything else?"

She frowned and half smiled and mixed it all together as an expression of confusion.

"I mean, off the top of my head . . . I'm pretty sure there might be hundreds of reasons. I just can't think of one right now."

"Neither can I. People get together for a whole lot of reasons, but the shorter the period of time they're together, the more precise the reason. Add into the equation the late hour, either I have to tell you something, you need to tell me something, I have to give you something, or you have to give me something. Prove me wrong."

"I can't, not off the top of my head."

A chill breeze moved her hair, and she shuddered. I rubbed my face with my hands. "Even if he was suddenly moved by the Holy Father to go and seek guidance from the prophet, that would still be an exchange of information. Even if Campbell's Great Uncle Johnny Walker had called Vargas and asked him to take James two hundred bucks as a belated birthday present, we are still looking at an exchange of physical objects."

"Okay, let's say, provisionally, that you're right. That he was here for an exchange of information or physical goods, or both. Where does that take us?"

"The next step is to decide what kind of exchange was most likely."

Her frown deepened. "And how do we do that?"

"We look at their common ground, at what links them. What are they most likely to exchange information about? What sort of goods are they most likely to exchange?"

She shook her head and pulled open the car door. "You're reaching, Stone."

"That's why I'm asking you to prove me wrong."

She climbed in the car, and I got in behind the wheel. She said, "Okay, what's their common ground? What are their links?"

I fired up the cat and sat for a moment thinking, letting the big engine idle. After a moment I asked her, "Do you take Campbell for a drug user?"

She didn't hesitate. "No. He is the pure warrior of Christ. I don't see him doing drugs."

I pulled away and headed north toward Morris Park Avenue. "What about coke?"

She looked surprised. Then she made a thoughtful face and looked straight ahead out of the windshield at the midmorning traffic. "Coke . . . If I'm honest . . ." She paused, sighed. "If I'm honest, I can see that. He has that inflated ego that often comes from regular use of coke. And I can see him rationalizing it as being necessary in order to do God's work."

I nodded. "So it's not hard to imagine Campbell calling Vargas, 'We need to talk, the cops have come to talk to me . . .' yadda yadda, as you might say, 'come and see me and on the way bring a few grams of coke.'"

"No, that's not hard to imagine."

"So we attach that information to the chief's application to Judge Petersen."

She pulled her phone from her pocket and dialed. She put it on speaker.

"Carmen!"

"Sir, we just heard from the team who've been tailing Nelson Vargas."

"Good. Any progress?"

"Yes, sir. Last night, quarter to twelve, Vargas left the Mescal Club and drove to James Campbell's church. Campbell has an apartment attached to the church. Vargas spent about thirty-five minutes with him, then left and returned to the Mescal Club. Sir, taken together with the fact that we can connect five of the six victims with both Vargas and Campbell, and given the fact that what brings the two of them together is their hatred of women . . ."

"I agree, Carmen. I think that is enough to take to Judge Petersen, and I think we stand a good chance of her signing off on a warrant to tap their telephone lines."

"Landlines and cells, sir."

"Of course."

"And emails and other media."

"All electronic forms of communication, Carmen."

"Thank you, sir."

"Anything else?"

She glanced at me. I shook my head.

"No, sir. With a bit of luck this might just swing it."

"Here's hoping, Carmen."

She hung up, and we sat in silence as we cruised down Morris Park toward White Plains.

"So now we need a progress report from O'Brien and Olvera," I said. "And I want to know what the hell is happening with our expert profiler from the bureau."

The answer to both questions was waiting for us when we arrived at the station a little more than half an hour later. O'Brien and Olvera had pulled up chairs to our desks and were busy writing a report together.

Dehan dropped into her chair while I pulled off my jacket and said, "What have you got?"

It was O'Brien who answered.

"George Allen is the only one who has credible alibis. He was in Rochester at the time of all six murders."

She handed us each a sheet of paper where each of the murders was listed, and alongside each one was Allen's alibi.

"You can see the details there," she said, "but in synthesis, he was either in meetings attended by board members and managers, or, in the case of Sharon Lipschitz and Maria Ortiz, he was traveling on the West Coast and has witnesses, bills, tickets, and credit card receipts to prove it. The rest are much shakier."

Olvera took over. His voice was startlingly deep.

"Reverend James Campbell can prove conclusively that he was preaching to a congregation in a rented hall on East 172nd Street at the time of Maria Ortiz's murder and at the time of Olga Hernandez's murder. For the rest"—he handed us each a sheet similar to the first—"he claims he was either preaching or in meetings with disciples, but we haven't been able to trace anyone who can corroborate those claims."

O'Brien took over again, handing out two more pieces of paper to me and to Dehan.

"That leaves Nelson Vargas and Golam Heitz. Heitz is in some ways the most problematic. Because he deliberately seeks to be alone, and the first thing his neighbors and acquaintances tell you about him is that he is a loner and they hardly ever see him. The guy is like clockwork, he rises at the same time every day and goes to bed at the same time every night. He does shift work, and will adjust automatically to each shift and slip immediately into his new routine. So his neighbors can confirm things like when he gets up, at what time he leaves and returns, and his workmates can confirm at what time he arrives and whether they saw him in the canteen, but what nobody can confirm for sure is where he was or what he was doing in between. And in all cases, from Mary Campbell right through to Claire Carter, it is feasible that he could have slipped away and made it to the scene of the crime and back again without his absence being noticed." She gave a reluctant smile. "He's the kind of guy you notice when he's there, but you don't notice when he ain't. In some cases, we've indicated on the list, the timing is tight, but in all the cases it is possible.

"Finally, Nelson Vargas. He relies entirely on the testimony of his gang members and the girls who work at his club, so in one sense his alibis are unbreakable, but equally they have a very poor credibility rating. You see on the list that each one is virtually identical: he was at the club, and he lists the people who were with him."

Dehan drew breath, but O'Brien preempted her.

"What you may find interesting, though, Detectives, is that where during Detective Alvarez's investigation five years back he used Jose Budia for all of his alibis, when we followed them up, he didn't name Jose in any of them."

Dehan made like the Cheshire cat and grinned. I leaned back in my chair and took a deep breath.

"That is very good work, very good work indeed."

We thanked them, and they left us at our desks, staring at each other. Finally, Dehan said, "So where does that leave us, Stone?"

I chewed my lip for a bit and gave my head a single shake.

"The fact that he faked his alibis tells us very little. That's like a knee-jerk reaction for him. Half the time he probably can't remember where he was at any given time or date because he's too stoned or drunk. But the fact that he has withdrawn Jose from his alibis is useful, because it means we can take those alibis to Jose and ask him, 'Are these alibis true or false,' and when he says, 'False,' that will confirm for the jury exactly what they will be suspecting."

She nodded. "Yeah, but it doesn't get us any closer to proving that Vargas and Campbell conspired to kill these girls."

"No, the connection with the girls is still tenuous at best."

"It's frustrating." She took a deep breath and held it. "It's frustrating that we can't get anything stronger than the fact that they crossed paths with these women, and it's frustrating that we can connect all of them except Sharon Lipschitz . . ."

I gave a few exaggerated nods and added, "And isn't that exactly what this guy does? Isn't that exactly what he did with the dates? Like we said before, he knows the cops are going to look for patterns of behavior to try and profile him, so he creates patterns and then breaks them: dates, kids, race, prostitution, sexual morality . . ."

She goggled at me. "You saying you think it's not him, but the perp is deliberately framing Vargas and Campbell?"

I smiled. "That would take some doing. But what I am saying is that it fits with the pattern of evidence he always leaves. And then there's the white Ford. Everything fits except one piece. I can't shake the feeling he is still playing us."

"Vargas hasn't got the brains for that. Campbell might, though."

I sighed and shook my head again. "It's just a feeling."

"Yeah?" She arched an eyebrow. "I trust your feelings, Stone."

"Yeah, me too."

And then the phone rang.

FIFTEEN

That feeling lingered. The call was from Saul Lipschitz.

"Detective Stone."

"Speaking."

"Dr. Saul Lipschitz."

Sentences were obviously not the big thing with Lipschitz.

"Good morning. Thanks for calling."

I heard a faint grunt. "How do you think I can help you?"

"We need to know more about your wife, Dr. Lipschitz, about her background, her private life..."

"Out of the question."

I put it on speaker and set my phone on the desk. Dehan leaned forward. I said, "What makes you say that, Dr. Lipschitz?"

"My wife's private life is none of your concern."

Dehan answered. "With all due respect, Dr. Lipschitz, you don't get to decide what is and isn't our concern."

"Who is that?"

"This is Detective Dehan, and the way it works, Doctor, is that witnesses don't get to decide what is and isn't relevant to our investigation."

"Dehan? You are impertinent, Detective Dehan."

His tone of voice sounded more amused than annoyed. Dehan's face said she wasn't all that amused. "On the contrary, Doctor. What I am saying is directly pertinent. Now, are you willing to help us find your wife's killer, or are you going to continue to be a damned *oysshteler*?"

I smiled at her, but her cheeks were flushed and her eyes were bright. She looked genuinely mad. There was a long moment's silence, then, "I fail to see how my wife's private life..."

I was getting bored so I interrupted. "Dr. Lipschitz, we have a couple of suspects, but we need to know how the killer came into contact with her in the first place."

"What do you mean, came into contact with her?"

I raised my eyes at Dehan. "I don't know how to put this without being blunt, Doctor? You're not making it easy. Clearly the killer selected Mrs. Lipschitz as a victim? So it stands to reason that before doing that, he must have become aware of her. So how did that happen? Did they shop at the same supermarket? Did they use the same dentist? Was she attending evening classes?"

"We had a housekeeper who took care of the household shopping. I very much doubt they used the same dentist, but I am happy to send you the contact details of our dentists. She was not attending evening classes. Anything else?"

Dehan stared at me a moment and then spoke in a tight voice.

"Dr. Lipschitz, it is very hard to escape the feeling that you are deliberately trying to conceal the killer's identity."

"That's absurd!"

"Is it? I am pretty sure that if we start investigating, we could find dozens of reasons why you might want to conceal the killer's identity. I have to tell you, Dr. Lipschitz, that in my experience, spouses who are reluctant to have the police investigate the murder of their husband or wife are hiding something, and often or not that something is the fact that they themselves murdered their partner..."

"How *dare* you!"

"Yeah, I dare, Doctor. Just like I dare to send a couple of cars over to the hospital to haul you in as a material witness and charge you with obstructing justice. I have to tell you that it stinks in my nostrils that we are trying to find your wife's killer, and all you give a damn about is avoiding scandal among your colleagues. Well that's tough, Doctor. We can do this the easy way or the tough way. You choose."

"You're threatening me."

I glanced at Dehan and smiled again. "Yes."

"You can't . . ."

"Dr. Lipschitz, I have a lot of work to do. I will do you the courtesy of trying to keep you and Sharon out of the media, but frankly I am getting bored with this conversation. Are you going to cooperate, or do I have to haul you in?"

He was quiet for a while, and I began to think he might have walked away, but then he said:

"What do you want to know?"

"Does the name James Campbell mean anything to you?"

"No. I don't know any James Campbell."

"What about Nelson Vargas?"

"No. Who are these people?"

"Did your wife ever speak to you about any religious sects? Did she ever show interest in any religious movements that struck you as peculiar?"

"Sharon was not especially religious. She was a practicing Jew, as am I. She was far more interested in day-to-day, practical issues than in abstract concepts of religion and philosophy."

"Was she a feminist?" It was Dehan.

The irritation was palpable in his voice. "What can that possibly have to do . . ."

I interrupted him. "Dr. Lipschitz. I assure you you are not the only busy person on the planet. We are trying to catch a serial killer who may, right now, be killing his seventh victim. Now do me a favor and answer the damned question. Was she a feminist?"

Another silence. "No. Like most intelligent people she was

aware of the disparities that exist, but she was not a feminist. Neither was she a submissive woman."

Dehan asked, "When you went out in the evening, did you always go together? Did she ever go out alone?"

"No, we always went out together."

"Have you heard of the Mescal Club, in the South Bronx?"

"Hardly!"

"It is very important that you answer this truthfully, Dr. Lipschitz. Is it possible that your wife ever went there, with girlfriends, work colleagues . . . ?"

"No. Absolutely not. And if she had, I would remember. It was a golden rule in our house: we go to bed together and we get up together, and we never go to bed angry. That was my grandfather's recipe for a happy marriage, and it worked. The idea of her going to a nightclub, especially in the Bronx, alone is preposterous."

"Dr. Lipschitz, where were you . . ."

"Dr. Hoffman told me you would ask this. The day Claire Carter was murdered I was in surgery from ten in the morning until six in the evening. I had my secretary make a list of the dates of the other Mommy's Boy murders and correlate them with my schedule at the time. I believe she has sent them to your email at the Forty-Third Precinct. I have no recollection of what I was doing, but she tells me I was either in surgery or at conferences in most cases, if not all. I am sorry I can't help you any more than that."

"What car do you drive, Dr. Lipschitz?"

"A Bentley, why?"

"Thank you for your help, Dr. Lipschitz. We'll be in touch if we need anything else."

I hung up and sat staring at Dehan, who was looking at the backs of her fingers. She shook her head, like she wasn't convinced they were her fingers at all, and said, "I think the technical term for what we are at the moment is 'screwed.'"

I grunted. "I was thinking of a shorter, Norse farming term."

She scowled at me. "You would. A Norse farming term?"

"Four letters, starts with an *F,* and means to plow and plant seeds."

"Seriously . . ."

"Yup, and I won't tell you what the furrow was called."

"Another four-letter word?"

"The Norse peoples were very brief and concise in how they expressed themselves, Dehan. But we are drifting off task here. What makes you say we are screwed? I found Dr. Lipschitz very helpful."

"Helpful . . ."

"Dare I say, plowing helpful."

"Care to explain?"

"Not really, except that what he has told us, surely, eliminates a whole swath of possibilities and leaves the true killer revealed in all his terrible nakedness."

"His, not their?"

I shrugged. "That of course is open to conjecture."

"Stone, are you going to be a pain in the ass again?"

"I just need to tidy up some details, Dehan. But I do believe if you think it through logically . . ."

She sighed. "I am thinking logically, Stone. Don't patronize me. This works one way and one way only: Campbell and Vargas conspired together to hunt and kill women. Campbell is the brains of the outfit, and Vargas is the muscle. They pick women either from Campbell's congregation or from their wider neighborhoods. There are four criteria: they must be plump, they must have a son, they must be happy and cheerful, and they must be whores. I am guessing they spend some time watching their prey and then one of them, I figure they take it in turns, moves in and makes the kill. I figure they use Campbell, as a man of the cloth, to gain entry, and Vargas takes care of the violence."

"What about the car?"

"The off-white Ford Kuga?"

"That car."

"It's Campbell's. He told us that."

I nodded. "Yes, he did. Okay, how about the fact that Sharon was very far from being what these apes would consider a whore?"

"I knew you'd ask that, and I have been wondering about it, but I get the impression Campbell would include all Jewish women under that general umbrella."

"You have thought this through. How about the fact that we can't connect Sharon with either Vargas or Campbell?"

"I grant you that is tricky, Stone, but not impossible. In fact, when you think it through, it actually makes sense."

"It does?"

"Yeah, smart-ass. She was the fourth of five, right?"

"Mm-hm." I nodded.

"They had already killed three women who were connected somehow to either Vargas or the church, or both. So Campbell proposes, following his system of creating patterns and then breaking them, that they should go and hunt a completely random woman who fits their basic criteria. She is a totally random victim. And, if I can go out on a limb here, the way he breaks patterns begins, itself, to form a pattern, a signature if you like. And this departure from the norm fits that pattern."

I raised my eyebrows and nodded. "That's smart, Dehan."

"So they go searching for a whore who is only a whore to them, and they select her at random in an area of the Bronx where they would not normally be active."

"Some very fine reasoning, Dehan. Now how do we prove it?"

"We need that tap."

"We do. So you are satisfied that all the other suspects are off the hook?"

She held up her left hand and counted them off, starting with her baby finger.

"Who have we got? Or, as you would say, whom? George Allen. We know his alibi is good. Golam Heitz, we know his alibis are weak, but we are also almost certain he could not, physically, have carried out the murders. That leaves us with Nelson and

Campbell. Okay, so Saul Lipschitz was briefly a suspect, but we've seen his alibis are watertight. Who else?"

The phone rang. I picked it up.

"John, it's John. Can you and Carmen come up here please?"

"We're on our way, sir." I hung up. "Chief wants to see us. I'm guessing it's about the warrant. You want to go on up? Tell him I'm on my way."

She frowned. "What are you going to do?"

"I'm curious about the car. I just want to look into something. It's probably nothing."

"Like hell!"

"The chief is waiting, Dehan. Mustn't keep the chief waiting. I'll be right up."

She narrowed her eyes at me and departed toward the stairs.

I made a couple of calls to a couple of PDs in the west and the north, sat thinking for a while, sent some emails, and then followed Dehan up. I found her in the inspector's office, leaning against the wall. There were two men in suits too. One of them had a fair beard turning to gray and very short hair, and a vaguely maritime look to him. The other was younger, darker, and slimmer and had college written all over him. They were sitting side by side on the sofa and could only have been Feds. They both stood and smiled and shook my hand when I came in. The chief spoke from behind his desk.

"John, these are Special Agents Trevellian and Panayotes." He indicated the beard and the student in turn. "Special Agent Panayotes is here to escort Jose Budia to the bureau. But I thought you might want a word with him before he does so."

I nodded. "Thank you, sir." I glanced at Dehan.

"Agent Panayotes," she said. "We see two areas of activity here. One is of primary interest to you, the other to us. We believe that Vargas, for the last five years, as well as being engaged in large-scale drug trafficking, has also been involved in serial killing, possibly with an accomplice.

"Now, obviously, we hope Jose Budia is going to provide you

with a lot of material on the Vargas operation, his bosses, and the network leading all the way back to Mexico. That's what he has promised us, and we believe it to be true.

"That's of interest to you, but what's of primary interest to us is any information relating to his possible activity as a serial killer."

Panayotes nodded. "That's why I have come along with Special Agent Trevellian." Trevellian smiled. Panayotes went on. "Doug has a PhD in criminology and psychology, and his specialist area is as a profiler in the field of serial killing. What we would like to do is liaise with you and Detective Stone through Special Agent Trevellian to see if we can take Vargas down in one coordinated operation."

Dehan nodded but didn't smile. "Swell. Our first concern is Vargas' alibis for the killings of Mommy's Boy's first five victims. Jose Budia was cited as a witness in all those alibis. But since we've taken Jose into custody, we have rechecked those alibis, and Vargas has not cited Jose in any of them."

Panayotes nodded serenely. "Sweet. So how do you want to do this? We want to cooperate as far as we can. You want to take that interrogation? You want us to deal with it and brief you? Or you want we should cooperate in the interrogation itself?"

I answered. "You take the interrogation. He'll be cooperative. We don't need any special strategy for this. Just get Jose to admit that the alibis were all fabricated, and if he can, to confirm where Vargas was on those days and at those times. He'll give you everything he's got. It's in his interest to put Vargas away for as long as possible. If he can nail him for a string of serial killings, he's guaranteed that Vargas will go away for life. He might even sleep at night. If you can let us have transcripts of any part of the interrogation that relates to the killings, the Church of the Holy Father and Son at the End of Days, or James Campbell, that will do fine."

Panayotes looked surprised. "You don't want in on the interrogations?"

Dehan spoke before I could answer. "I do."

I ignored the comment and went on speaking. "No, I don't want to delay your operation. Vargas is probably already scrambling to limit the damage Jose can do. What I am interested in, if we are going to cooperate, is the kind of surveillance you guys can do, and we simply haven't the resources. Vargas has a tight, rather strange relationship with Reverend James Campbell. He went to see him last night at about midnight, stayed for half an hour, and then returned to the Mescal Club. We can watch him." I glanced at the chief. "We may even be able to tap his phone, but I don't know how much that is going to give us. But you guys"—I pointed at Panayotes—"you guys can get inside and hear their conversations. I think Reverend James Campbell might surprise us all."

Special Agent Doug Trevellian made an interested face. "What makes you say that?"

I shrugged. "In my experience people don't visit each other at midnight for just half an hour unless they are having a really speedy affair, unless they are exchanging goods of some sort, or unless they are exchanging information. Neither of the two struck me as gay, so it's my opinion that a tap on both their phones, and a few strategically placed bugs in Campbell's house, could reveal vital information about what exactly they were exchanging."

Dehan, who was beginning to look pissed, said, "It could reveal information about their next intended target."

I added, "Or their next delivery."

Panayotes spent the next twenty minutes explaining to us the various ways the bureau had of getting bugs inside the Reverend James Campbell's dwelling. After that I asked him if he could give us a profile of Mommy's Boy.

He said he could.

SIXTEEN

Special Agent Doug Trevellian had a deep, rich, friendly voice. He kept a pipe in his pocket, which he pulled out and used as a prop when speaking. He didn't light it. He just held it cupped in his hand and gestured with it.

"I have to say straightaway that I very much doubt that Mommy's Boy is a conspiracy of two. It is extremely rare for serial killers to work in pairs, and when they have in the past it has usually been teams of a man and a woman, as in Myra Hindley and Ian Brady, Paul Bernardo and Karla Homolka, a few others, but male teams are extremely rare. I can only think of three offhand: Wolfgang Abel and Marco Furlan. There was Dean Corll, who enlisted the help of Henley and Brooks, and then there were Henry Lucas and Ottis Toole. And none of those profiles really fit the murders we are looking at here."

I frowned. "How's that?"

"For a very simple reason, Detective Stone. The ritual nature of the murders expresses the fantasy and the obsession of one man, a man who is obsessed with his mother. On the rare occasions when you get serial killers working in teams, what you usually find is that one acts as a kind of 'Igor' figure, serving the other and in some cases procuring the victims for him. But in this case the victims are killed in their own homes—there is no procuring.

"Typically, when we find a serial killer who is the victim of a mother obsession, he will be rather weak or underdeveloped physically. Possibly in his childhood he was not allowed to develop normally, as a boy. Perhaps his mother was smothering, by turns overmothering and excessively cold, cruel, or judgmental. His father will have been absent, either through his work, through divorce, or even death.

"This man is possessed of an overwhelming need to punish his mother. In removing her breasts and stabbing her in the womb he is robbing her of her womanhood. He does not believe she is entitled to her womanhood. He probably believes he has been betrayed by his mother and several other women. So this man will be a misogynist, and his main complaint about women will be that they are not entitled to the praise they receive, that they cannot be trusted, that they are faithless, and, particularly in view of the victims he has chosen, he will view them as whores. The love he believed he was entitled to from his mother was, no doubt, given to one or more men whom he hated because they displaced him. But the blame, ultimately, he reserves for his mother.

"But"—he smiled at his pipe here, like they were sharing a private joke—"and here is where it gets a little complicated. Our killer is wracked by guilt. There is a deeper level to his cutting off her breast and stabbing her in the womb. Note he does not rape any of his victims. Though he is robbing them of their womanhood, he is also denying himself the love he does not believe he is entitled to. He feels betrayed by his mother, deeply so, but he also believes he has let her down. He was not good enough to earn her love.

"Typically this woman would have chosen rather brutish men, ignorant but animalistically male. And he, having been cosseted and mothered to the point of becoming rather weak and even frail, would have felt extremely inadequate compared to these men whom his mother loved and gave herself to. He may, perhaps, even come across as a little effeminate, but I doubt he is homosexual.

"Age, I would put at early to midthirties, probably soft-spoken, retiring, unimposing, shy, scared of women, scared of very masculine men, something of an underachiever, though I would say of slightly above-average intelligence. He fails to achieve through lack of self-confidence and drive, not through lack of ability. He likes to play games of strategy and fancies himself as more intelligent than he really is. There is a secret arrogance to the man. Though he is crippled by a lack of belief in himself, he will, in times of crisis, resort to his own inner fantasy world where he is supremely arrogant and powerful. He has the power of life and death in his hands, in his fantasy world."

Dehan cleared her throat. "Can you shed any light on why he stopped killing suddenly, and then started again?"

He puffed out his cheeks. "It is very hard to say. There could be numerous reasons, Detective Dehan. My own feeling, and I stress it is a feeling, is that he did not stop. I believe you have made inquiries of other PDs and the bureau, and I believe you will start to get reports shortly, as the request works its way through the system, of similar murders in at least one other state."

She nodded. "So you think he simply moved and became active elsewhere."

"I would have thought that was a pretty safe bet. He may have moved because of work, but whatever work he does, his job will not involve close contact with the public, because he only feels strong and confident when he is in his fantasy world. When he is brought back to reality, he feels inadequate, he may stammer, he may be clumsy, or he might hide behind a front of curt bad manners and ill temper. Whatever device he uses, he avoids contact with the public.

"Which in turn leads us to two other points. He is unlikely to be married or have a family, unless he has found a wife who was willing to join him in his reclusive state, which is rare. It also means that he is unlikely to find his victims through work. It's not impossible, but it is unlikely. He would need to be in a position where he was able to see them, without having contact with them.

"Much more likely is that when he is alone, say after work or on the weekends, he enters into his fantasy state and then goes hunting. His victims are not just a physical type; there are also important character traits which he observes and homes in on, like their bubbly, fun nature. And there are personal details like the fact that they have at least one son. So this tells us he goes hunting, selects a victim, and stalks her until he has gathered all the information he needs."

Dehan cleared her throat.

"I wanted to ask you about this. All the victims except Sharon Lipschitz were . . ." She hesitated and glanced at the chief. "They were borderline sex workers, small-time prostitutes, which we thought qualified them, for him, as whores, and that brought them within the profile of his victims. But Sharon was not, by any stretch of the imagination, a whore. Unless he was anti-Semitic and all Jewish . . ." Special Agent Trevellian was already shaking his head.

"No, don't get confused, and don't confuse your terms of reference. If he had the view that all Jewish women were by definition whores, all his victims would have been Jewish. That isn't how it works. He is not going to go out looking for a woman who fits his definition of a whore, and think, 'Oh, I can't find one, I'll settle for a Jew.' No, not at all. What is far more likely is one of two scenarios.

"One: for him, the act of prostitution is not the trigger, the trigger is the lively, bubbly personality, which he sees as flirting and inviting men to have sex. Now, if five out of six of his victims, that we know of, were prostitutes, then it may be that their lively, bubbly personality was part of what they used to attract clients—the way some salesmen do. And the sixth had that same personality but was not a prostitute. Whore is a very emotional word, and it does not always mean a prostitute.

"Two: the choice of victims has nothing to do with prostitution. You have probably noticed that he starts what appears to be a trend or a pattern, and then breaks it. He may be playing with you, and if that's the case we have a problem, because at this stage it is impossible to tell what is actual profile and what is moonshine."

I said, "Is that what you think happened with Sharon Lipschitz—it was a deliberate shift of profile?"

He shook his head and examined his pipe for a moment. "No." He shook his head again and raised his eyes to look at me. "No, because the shift is not significant enough to confuse or to throw you off his scent if you were on it. No, I think the fact of prostitution was never a major factor. What is a major factor is a woman who is attractive to men and who has the kind of personality that welcomes the attention." He pointed at the inspector. "I have given your chief three copies of my report. But I would like to be involved in the investigation, both on our side and, above all, on yours, so that I can refine my profile as more data becomes available."

I took a deep breath and sighed, nodding as I did so. "Sure, but I'm afraid we have been focusing increasingly on Vargas and Campbell as coconspirators, and I have to say that a lot of the evidence points at them. But neither of them fits your profile."

He nodded for a bit and then made a face like he'd bitten into a lemon. "I have to tell you, Detective Stone, I know you've only had the case a couple of days, but I've studied the case file from the time when Detective Alvarez took it to the point of your last report, and I honestly don't believe that your killer is among your suspects." I smiled, and he held up both hands. "Profiling is not an exact science, Detective Stone, and God help us if it ever becomes one, but that would have to be my informed opinion as things stand."

I turned to the chief. "Do we have the warrant to tap Campbell's and Vargas' phones?"

He nodded. "We do, and as you might expect it's pretty extensive. We are authorized to use taps and bugs and to surveil their phone calls and their electronic communications as well as their personal conversations. Just before you came up, we were discussing with Agent Panayotes that the bureau is better placed to introduce the bugs into the club, as well as Campbell's private apartments."

"Yeah, sure, that's great. I'd like O'Connor and Brightman to share in the monitoring of conversations." I turned to Panayotes. "If that's okay with the bureau?"

"Yeah," he rumbled. "No problem. We're detailing a team now to set up the equipment and plant the bugs. Tell your men to contact me and we'll brief them in."

The chief spread his hands. "Anything else? I think we've covered everything..."

I shook my head, and Panayotes got to his feet. He smiled at Dehan. "I'm taking Budia to Broadway now. You want to come along? We'll have round one with him as soon as we get there."

She looked at me. I said, "Call me when you're done. I'll come and get you."

She nodded, and they left together. Trevellian and I followed a couple of minutes later. On the stairs I asked him, "How deeply psychotic is this guy likely to be?"

He stopped on the stairs with his hands in his pockets and stared down at the floor, while cops in uniforms streamed and jostled around us.

"I'm not sure," he said at last, "that he is psychotic at all. Or even that we can apply the usual terms of psychosis and neurosis to this phenomenon. But if I had to . . ." He started walking again, still with his hands in his pockets, down toward the main entrance and the detectives' room.

"If I had to, I'd say that very few serial killers are truly psychotic. It is possible that they are deeply neurotic, and that their obsession with killing peaks more or less periodically, and when it does, it spills over into a psychotic episode while they kill." He shrugged and sighed. "This is not an area of psychology like any other. The dynamics of the mind in a serial killer are not understood, and that isn't helped by the fact that serial killers themselves vary so widely."

We stopped outside the entrance, and through the open door I saw Dehan climbing into a dark blue Audi with Panayotes. Jose and two guys in suits were climbing into a Chevy beside it. Trevellian kept talking.

"Some experts define a serial killer as simply somebody who has killed more than three people consecutively. For me that is too legalistic and misses the point that true serial killers kill because they want to, not because they believe they need to in order to achieve some practical end, like money or vengeance."

I nodded as I watched the two cars pull away. I spoke absently.

"In murder the motive creates the desire to kill." I smiled ruefully at him. "If you die, I inherit from Dad, so that makes me want to kill you. But in the serial killer the desire to kill *is* the motive."

"Correct. That simple fact means to me that they are a whole class of killer unto themselves, quite distinct from almost ninety percent of murderers."

"I agree. So, your opinion is that this is a guy working alone, that he may be neurotic in as much as he is obsessed with killing, but that most of the time he is apparently rational, though he might from time to time slip into psychotic episodes, when he is alone."

"Yes, that would be an accurate assessment. And he is probably in a psychotic episode when he is killing."

I watched him leave and walked back to my desk with my hands deep in my pockets, echoing Trevellian's stance moments before. I dropped into my chair, shook my mouse, and checked my emails. There was one from my contact at the DMV, the girl I'd contacted before going up to the chief's office. It said:

Hi John, this is what I could find for New York:

Ford Kuga, cream, NY license plates (XXXXX), registered last September 22nd.

1969 MG BGT, racing green, Los Angeles plates (XXXXX), registered 31st April, 2015.

Hope that helps.

Susanne

IT HELPED.

Now I knew who he was, and I knew that Trevellian had got it half right. But this guy was smarter than anyone had given him credit for, and he had led the bureau's profiler on the same kind of wild goose chase he'd led Alvarez. His real skill, his genius, was at presenting himself as somebody he was not, and at making people believe in him. He was an Iago, an empty space which he could fill with any identity he cared to produce at the time; a towering ego that felt it had the right to take people's lives at will, and yet displayed a complete absence of identity.

SEVENTEEN

I sat for a long time, thinking. Then I spent twenty minutes on Google Earth, examining the Bronx, and in particular Castle Hill Avenue. After that I climbed in my car and drove over to the Church of the Holy Family, and Claire Carter's house. The house was still sealed with police tape, which hung listless and oddly sad in the dull light and gave desultory slaps on the wooden door, like a beaten fighter who hasn't the strength to surrender.

I didn't go to Claire's house. I went instead to Edna Brown's place and rang on the bell. She appeared at the door after a couple of minutes, dabbing her mouth with a napkin.

I smiled an apology at her, which she took cautiously. "I am sorry to intrude, Edna. I just need to ask you a question, maybe two."

"So long as you don't mind asking while I'm eating."

"Not at all. And I won't keep you more than a minute."

I followed her through to the dining area beside her open-plan kitchen, where she was eating a steak with mashed potatoes. She gestured me to the seat opposite her own and sat.

"If I was twenty years younger, I'd offer you food and drink. But one of the pleasures of growing old is you don't have to pretend anymore. What did you forget to ask me last time you were here?"

I leaned back and crossed one leg over the other.

"You said that you were expecting Claire at around eleven that morning, you remember."

She nodded with her mouth full. "I do."

"And you said you didn't remember seeing any men going in."

She smiled and shrugged, spreading her hands, still holding the knife and fork. "If I had, I would have known not to expect her."

"Sure. I was just wondering about women, though. Did you see any women arrive that morning?"

She frowned and set down her knife and fork.

"I hope you're not suggesting what I think you're suggesting . . ."

I shook my head. "I'm not suggesting anything, Edna. I'm investigating a murder, and I need to know whether you noticed a woman arrive that morning, before eleven."

She looked past me, gazing out the window at the dull street in the gray light.

"Well, now that you mention it, there was. I think she was a Jehovah's Witness or one of those crazy sects. She was a little frumpy in her dress, with a felt hat and a handful of leaflets."

"Black or white?"

"Um . . ." She hesitated and gave an embarrassed laugh. "You know, I'm not sure. The hat and the coat and the collar, and she was wearing glasses . . . I think she was white, but I wouldn't swear to it."

"You spoke to her?"

"No! When I saw the threat of somebody telling me the good news I legged it into the kitchen."

"Now, how about the white Ford SUV? Was it already there?"

She sank back in her chair. "Well, my goodness. Do you know, I think it was . . ."

"And what time would that have been?"

"Well, I had gone out to get the post. So it must have been about nine thirty. I have a very fixed routine, Detective Stone. Certainly it was between nine fifteen and nine thirty-five."

"So, would you describe this woman as being basically nondescript?"

She was amused by that and chuckled.

"Yes, I suppose I would. Late twenties to midthirties, average height, build..." She shrugged. "Yes, nondescript."

I thanked her and stepped outside. The temperature had dropped a few degrees, and it had started to spit with rain. I pulled up my collar and shoved my hands in my pockets, and walked the two hundred yards over the Castle Hill overpass, with the Cross Bronx Expressway humming under my feet.

On the other side of the bridge was the Sunoco gas station. I strolled in past the pumps and pushed into the store. There was a guy behind the counter counting coins. He looked like it was the most important thing he was ever likely to do in his life. I let him get to ten before I showed him my badge.

"Detective Stone, NYPD."

He glanced at me and made it to twenty before he said, "I didn't call the cops."

"Well I guess it's your lucky day, they came anyway. You the manager?"

"Yeah."

"You here every day midweek?"

Now he was making stacks of ten. "Yeah."

"Keep counting those coins and I might sneeze and blow the whole damn lot all over the floor. And by the way, you got a license for cockroaches? I think I saw five over by the sandwiches there."

He looked at me the way a man might look at the pain in his ass.

"What?"

"Were you here Tuesday morning?"

"Yeah, I'm here every morning, 'cept Sunday. Sunday I don't work."

"I need to see the CCTV for Tuesday morning."

"You got a warrant?"

"No, but I can come back with one when I come back with the sanitary inspection officer and Vice. Or, if I'm lucky, you'll turn out to be a citizen with a civic conscience."

He sighed heavily and gazed at his coins. He looked like Napoleon about to tell Josephine, "Not tonight."

He called his employee to tend shop, and I followed him to his office in back. There he pulled the video footage on his PC and said, "What time you want to look at?"

I jabbed my thumb at the door like I was hitchhiking.

"Scram. I'll call you if I need a cup of coffee."

He grunted and left. I sat in the chair and studied the still on the screen. I could see the gas pumps, the parking lot, and Castle Hill Avenue ahead. I scrolled to eight o'clock and watched the traffic pass in a slow, jerky procession, with occasional vehicles filtering off and stopping at the pumps.

At eight o'clock I saw a white or off-white Ford Kuga roll past, headed south. I fast-forwarded to just before noon and let it play. At ten minutes past twelve, a cream Ford Kuga rolled into the gas station from the direction of the Church of the Holy Family and Claire Carter's house on Watson Avenue. It pulled up at a pump and a man got out. He was wearing a hat and sunglasses. He filled up the car, then disappeared from view.

I froze the image and switched to the indoor cameras. All you could see here was that he was average height, wearing a beige jacket and a cowboy-style hat. He paid cash and left.

The outdoor camera told me that he got back in and drove away. I selected the front view camera and saw the registration plate. It was the same one Susanne had sent me.

I pulled my cell from my pocket and called Dispatch.

"I need a BOLO on a cream or off-white Ford Kuga, New York plates . . ." I gave her the registration and went on, "Driver might be male or female, of average height and average build, black or white."

"You kidding me?"

"I wish."

There was no point calling for a forensic team. Too many people had passed through the station and handled the pump, but I stepped out of the office and found Mr. Happy again.

"Have you banked Tuesday morning's money yet?"

He looked at me slack-jawed for a moment. "No, tomorrow."

"I need all the footage for Tuesday, and I need the cash you took on Tuesday at midday."

"What?"

"This is a homicide investigation, and you really don't want a charge of obstructing justice on this particular case. Now, we can do this nicely, or I can close the station. You choose."

"Okay, okay, I'll get you the video footage and the parcel of cash. Each day is set aside . . ."

He hurried off like an urgent mouse, mumbling to himself. I followed and called Joe.

"Stone, how's it hanging?"

"Perpendicular. I'm going to send over some video footage and a parcel of money."

"Nice."

"The person who appears in the footage is, I am ninety-nine percent sure, Mommy's Boy."

The manager looked up from his desk and goggled at me. I pointed at the computer. He went back to work.

"Holy cow, Batman! You sure?"

"Like I said, ninety-nine percent sure. What I am not sure about is, well, whether it's a man or a woman, whether he or she is black or white, or anything else for that matter, except that this person is of average height and build and nondescript."

"Are you serious?"

"Yeah, he-she-it is wearing clothes that mask virtually all features, and the one witness I have says she isn't sure whether the person she saw was black or white. So what we need is some very serious video enhancement. Now, the good news is, I have a bundle of money, and among that money is the money with which our suspect paid for his or her gas."

"That is going to be a hell of a job, especially if we don't have a sample to compare it with, and we can't eliminate all the other, legitimate prints."

I nodded, like he could see me. "Yeah, I know. I'll see what I can do."

I hung up and left him sounding confused, then stepped over to where the manager was uploading the footage onto a pen drive.

"You remember this guy?"

He stared at the image on the screen for a moment. "Yeah, kind of."

"Did he speak?"

"Nah."

"Was it a man or a woman?"

"I thought it was a man, the way he was dressed, but now you asked . . ." He shrugged. "I'm not sure."

He gave me the USB drive and the parcel of money, stuffed into a plastic groceries bag, and I made my way back to where I had parked my car. I dumped the stuff in the trunk and called Dehan.

I had to ring three times and finally she answered.

"Yeah, what is it. I was in the interrogation."

"You going to join the Feds now? When you said you were thinking of taking a different job, I didn't think you meant that."

"Cut it out, Stone. What do you want?"

"I know who did it, and I think I can prove it."

"You serious?"

"What do you think? You think you can pull yourself away from your new friends and come and give me a hand?"

"Are you jealous, Stone?"

"Truthfully, when I saw you climbing in the car with Panayotes, a little."

"Good, come and get me. I'm all yours, big boy."

"I'm on my way."

But I had to go first to the station and have a bike run the evidence over to Joe. So it was another half hour before I set off for Manhattan. I called Dehan again from the car. It rang till her answering service kicked in. I rang again four more times with the same result. So I called Bernie.

"John, you owe me three thousand and fifty-six beers."

"I'll buy them all for you today if you find Carmen for me."

"You'll have to explain that to me, pal. Last I heard you were married to the poor girl."

"Yeah, she was kidnapped by some Feds who took her to the field office to sit in on the interrogation of Jose Budia . . ."

"Oh, you guys are in on that? That's just upstairs. You want me to go fetch her for you?"

"I'd be grateful, Bernie. She's not answering her phone."

He hung up and called back five minutes later as I was crossing the Bronx River and heading south toward Woodstock.

"Who was she with? Special Agent Panayotes and his crew?"

"Yeah."

"They said she left right after you called her. I'm going to go down, see if she's waiting in the lobby. She might have gone to get a sandwich."

"Sure, thanks, Bernie."

I hung up with a hot twist of anxiety in my gut. Getting a sandwich didn't prevent you from answering your phone, and he knew it. I hit the gas and started weaving in and out of the traffic, finding spaces where I could and harvesting a cacophony of horns and Klaxons behind me.

He called again as I was peeling off onto East 135th Street.

"Stone, she's not here. We've put out a BOLO and we're about to track her GPS on her phone. We've got guys down in the Plaza trying to find anyone who saw her or what happened."

"You calling her?"

"No, John. If something's happened to her and it keeps ringing, they might switch it off."

"Yeah, okay."

"You gonna keep a cool head?"

"Screw you."

"That's what I thought. She needs you cool and efficient."

"I know. I'll be there in ten."

I moved down Broadway too fast, closing on the Federal Plaza. As I approached, I could see Bernie on his cell waving at me from the sidewalk, stepping into the traffic. I pulled up beside him, leaned over, and wound down the window. He leaned in.

"We've got her GPS. She's on the move. The guy at Dunkin' Donuts says he saw a hot Latina in jeans and a leather jacket waiting on the sidewalk maybe twenty minutes ago. He saw a Chevy van with tinted windows pull up. She spoke to whoever was inside and got in."

"That was Dehan. Where is she right now?"

He opened the door and climbed in. "Willis Avenue Bridge. Move!"

I swore violently under my breath, and as he slammed the door I accelerated south toward Park Row. "It's going to take us twenty minutes to get there. She could be dead by then."

The Jag held the road as I cornered and accelerated toward Frankfort Street and the FDR.

Bernie was staring about him. "Haven't you got a siren in this thing?"

"No."

"Jesus!"

The exclamation might have been for the absence of a siren, or it might have been the surge of power that crushed him back into his seat as I floored the pedal in third, rammed in fourth, and engaged the overdrive. I saw the needle inch to a hundred and ten and then crawl up toward a hundred and twenty. Compared to modern supercars it wasn't much, but compared to the saloons cruising at fifty along the FDR it was enough. The cat snarled, and we weaved dangerously among the Toyotas, the Fords, Jeeps, and Chevys, hurtling past them and leaving them shrinking in my rearview.

"How old is this damned thing?"

"Sixty. Where is she now?"

Horns blared and made with the Doppler effect as we screamed past them. Bernie checked his cell as we hurtled under the Williamsburg Bridge.

"Joining the Bruckner Boulevard, headed east. We're gaining on them."

I growled, "Of course we are."

"Have you got a plan?"

"You don't want to hear it." I grabbed my radio and called Dispatch. I gave my name and badge number, then said:

"In pursuit of a dark Chevy van with tinted windows. I believe Detective Carmen Dehan is a hostage in the van. Requesting all vehicles fall back and keep their distance. Detective Dehan's life could be at risk."

He closed his eyes and sighed. "We never had this conversation. Just don't make me a witness."

I didn't answer. Seven minutes later we thundered over the bridge onto the Bruckner Boulevard. There were no patrol cars visible.

"Where are they?"

"Crossing the Bronx. You're two or three minutes away and closing. We should see them soon."

We danced through the traffic, swinging from lane to lane wherever there was an opening. After two minutes Bernie pointed, but I had already seen it.

"That van! Fifteen cars, fourteen cars ahead."

"I see it."

"Slow down!"

I slipped past five, six, seven more cars and positioned myself six cars behind the target, slowing as I went.

"What are you going to do, John?"

"I thought you didn't want to know."

"I'm not asking, you're not telling. This car isn't bugged, and I dream about Dehan leaving you and marrying me. So cut the crap and tell me what you plan to do!"

"See where they take her. That will tell me who they are and what I have to do next."

They came off at the Bronx River Parkway and turned down Soundview Avenue. I let them get ahead and followed at a discreet distance. At Lafayette they turned east and my cell rang. It was Dehan's phone calling. I grabbed it.

"Yeah."

"Hey, pig. You know who this is?"

"It's Detective Dehan's phone. Who are you?"

"Oh, you don't know? I'm your wife's new man. She's here with me now in my love mobile. We gonna make some sweet love, Latino style, real soon. She gonna call me *papito*. She ever call you *papito,* pig?"

My belly was on fire and I felt sick, but I couldn't afford to give in to the feelings. I said, "What do you want?"

He laughed. "Right now, I want your wife, pig. She is super hot, man. I'll call you and tell you what I want after I have had my fill."

He hung up. Bernie said, "Does he know we're with him?"

"He can't not know. He's left her cell on so we'll follow. He wants to negotiate."

"Who is it?"

"It's Vargas. He wants Jose."

EIGHTEEN

I called the chief.

"John, what . . ."

"Vargas has abducted Dehan."

"Dear God!"

"Listen to me. I'm pretty sure he's taking her to Campbell's church on Castle Hill . . ."

"The Father, the Son and the End of Days. So Dehan was right!"

"Once they get there, they are going to use her as a hostage, and they are going to demand we hand Jose over to them, and, I would guess, safe passage to Mexico."

"Yes, that makes sense."

"But the Feds are going to bring in one of their hotshot negotiators, and this could turn into a Waco, and every hour that she is in there is an hour of risk where she could get raped, tortured, or murdered."

He was silent for three long seconds. Then he said, "What are you driving at, Stone?"

"I'm going to go in there and bring her out."

"I absolutely cannot authorize that."

"Sir, it makes no difference whether you authorize it or not.

Dehan . . . We think Dehan is pregnant. I am not going to leave my wife and child in the hands of those animals while we observe protocol."

His voice was barely a whisper. "Dear God . . . John, if you get killed . . ."

"I'll make sure not to, sir. I can't afford to."

As I had expected, the van slowed at the intersection with Castle Hill and turned south. At Homer Avenue it turned left and pulled into the parking lot at the back of the church. I turned into the gas station and auto repair opposite the church and parked out of sight.

I sat a moment, trying to work out the best way to do something that had no right way of being done. That was when my cell rang again.

"Hey, pig, you wanna hear your bitch scream?"

I answered fast. "Let's get one thing straight from the start. The first time she screams, SWAT moves in with flash-bangs and assault rifles and you all die. No negotiation, no warning. And if you come out alive, I will personally ensure you face trial in a state that still has the death penalty. From here to Arizona via Texas, there has to be some body with your prints on it. Whether there is or there isn't, you can be sure I'll find it. She just needs to scream once, Vargas."

I put it on speaker and glanced at Bernie. Vargas was speaking.

"Yeah, I am standing in a puddle of my own piss, I am so scared. Now listen to me, pig. You wanna see your bitch alive, you gonna bring me Jose, then you are gonna arrange an air taxi to take me and my boys to Mexico, to Obregón. You got two hours. In one hundred and twenty-one minutes, I am gonna gang-rape your bitch, and after that I am gonna start cutting off her toes and her fingers. Two hours, starting now."

He hung up.

I pulled the Sig P226 from under my arm and cocked it. Bernie shook his head.

"What the hell are you going to do?"

I looked him straight in the eye and lied. "I'm going to offer myself as a hostage instead of Dehan, so I can feed information to the SWAT team."

"That's stupid, John. They'll hold you both and they'll remove your cell..."

He was talking and he was watching my eyes, and he knew I was bullshitting him. His voice trailed off. I said, "We're wasting time. You'd better contact the bureau and call in SWAT."

I crossed the gas station and loped across the road to the church, then walked up to the front door. There was a printed sign that said the services had been cancelled for the day, but there were no guys waiting with automatic weapons. They'd be waiting for me inside. I hesitated for just a second, then I walked up and pushed through the large, plate glass doors. They came at me from both sides, fast, with their weapons held out in front of them.

The guy on my right had a rattler tattooed across his face, sliding from one cheek across his forehead and down the other side. He had a crew cut and crazy eyes. He was small and wiry and held a Glock 17 in both hands, pointed at my head.

The one on my left was fat. He had a Sancho Panza moustache and no tattoos on his face, but his arms and chest were smothered in them. His eyes were about as crazy as his friend's. He said, "Don moof! Raise your hands." I put them up. To his pal he said, "*Cubrelo...*"—*cover him*.

My heart was pounding high in my chest. I was terrified. I knew I could die at any moment. But what terrified me most was what could happen to Dehan if I died. And that kind of terror can make you either overcautious or reckless, and sometimes you need to be reckless in order to survive.

Sancho closed in behind me and started patting me down. The Rattler closed in a step too, staring hard into my eyes. I knew from this moment on I would be dragged tighter into their control. What I did next I had never practiced. I had only ever seen it done on YouTube, but I knew the moment had to be when he found my Sig under my arm.

His hand fell on it and he reached for it. In that moment I slammed my hands together. My right smashed into his wrist. My left grabbed the barrel of his Glock and levered it in toward his face. It happened in one fluid movement in less than a second. Then my right index finger was over his and I pulled the trigger.

The slug punched a hole in his chest. His friend was still peering over my shoulder into the Rattler's startled face when I turned to face him. He rushed me, stumbled over his pal, and fell against me. We lost balance, and as we went down he was staring up into my face with wide, terrified eyes.

We hit the ground, and he was clawing at my gun hand with his nails, making a strange noise through his teeth and his lips. He was heavy, and I was having trouble breathing. But some basic common sense in my head told me he was fixated on his pal's Glock, so as he clawed at my hand, I flipped the weapon away. It hit the wooden floor and slid a few feet.

He scrambled off me and clawed his way after it. I was trembling like crazy but I managed to get on one knee and pull the Sig from under my arm. His hand was on the Glock, and I shot him in the ear. He went still.

I could hear my own breathing rasping and trembling in my chest. I was shaking badly, but I got to my feet and ran toward the chapel. There was no sign of Vargas or Campbell or any of Vargas' men.

I shouldered the swinging doors to the chapel and burst in, expecting to be riddled with bullets, but not knowing what else to do. I needn't have worried. The chapel was empty. My heart was racing hard. I could feel my mind on the brink of panic. But a cold voice in my head told me the chapel was too easy to storm. They'd be upstairs, in Campbell's apartment.

Where?

I ran down the aisle and scrambled onto the stage. At the back, on the left, there was a door, painted white like the walls that supported the great cross. I tried the handle, and it opened. I was in a short passage carpeted in red with white walls. A dogleg at the end led out of sight. I followed the passage with the Sig held out in front of me and turned the corner. There was a broad flight of stairs that led up to a small landing with a single red door on the right.

I sprinted up the steps and paused in front of the door with my back against the wall.

They had kept Dehan's GPS activated, and they must have known that we would follow it. They wanted that much so they could negotiate. But did they know I would come in alone, without the SWAT team? That was unlikely. They would expect the cops to follow procedure and enter into negotiations.

I aimed at the lock and put two rounds through it, then I kicked the door and burst in.

I was in a very spacious, open-plan room. Over on the right was a kitchen with a breakfast bar and bare, redbrick walls. Over on the left there was an open fireplace big enough for a tall man to stand inside. To either side of it were tall stained glass windows, and ranged around it were leather armchairs and a sofa set on what looked like very expensive rugs on a bare, wooden floor.

Campbell was sitting in one of the armchairs, frowning at me. Leaning against the wall, with his arms crossed, also frowning at me, was Vargas. And halfway between me and them were two guys in denim jackets with the sleeves torn off and their arms covered in tattoos. They were Cabras, and they were holding AK-47s and pointing them right at me.

On the floor, bound and gagged, was Dehan, and her eyes told me she was terrified.

Long seconds of silence passed. Then, with sudden violence, Vargas burst out laughing. It was a noisy, ugly laugh that would have suited a spotty fourteen-year-old better than this thirty-year-old psychopath.

I lined him up in my sights and knew I could kill him right then. He pushed off the wall and started walking toward me.

"You crazy son of a bitch." His voice was mild, even agreeable. "You really are an old-school dinosaur, huh? A real live Dirty Harry. You come bustin' in here with a semiautomatic, like you gonna save the world. I should let Guaco and Quique turn you into a fockin' colander right now."

He stopped beside the gorilla he'd called Guaco and chuckled.

"We gonna make spaghetti later, and we can use you to drain the water, right? You gonna have so many fockin' holes in you. But I'm figurin' if I call the papers and the TV channels, and I tell them we got the dynamic duo here, hosband an' wife who clear up all the cold cases, both of them beautiful, right? The whole fockin' nation is gonna fall in love with you and *nobody* is gonna want to see you executed by the bad ol' Sinaloa boys, right. The political pressure to get you released is gonna be real heavy for the mayor and the governor and everybody from there on down. Am I wrong?"

He turned to the gorilla. "*Péguele un tiro en la rodilla.*"

Dehan screamed through her gag and I knew it was bad. I acted without thinking. I'm a pretty good marksman, but I was truly motivated too, and I put a slug right through the gorilla's forehead. The last thing I saw of him was his eyes rolling up in his head as he keeled over backward.

By then I was running and screaming, heading straight for the other gorilla called Quique. I remember his eyes big and wide. I remember him raising his assault rifle and pointing it at my face. I was still screaming when I dropped to my knees and slid along the bare, polished boards as the burst of molten lead tore above my head.

The Sig was still in my hands, held out in front of me. I pulled the trigger twice and both rounds tore into the poor bastard's lower belly. He screamed like a girl and fell to the ground clutching what was left of his genitals as a huge pool of blood expanded around him.

I clambered to my feet and ran, but I was too late. Campbell had got to his feet, and in two strides he was standing over Dehan.

He lowered himself so that one knee was on her neck. In his hand he held a kitchen knife.

Vargas joined him, looking at his two dead men.

"You one dangerous son of a bitch, Detective Stone." He pulled a Glock 19 from his waistband and pointed it at me. He went to speak a couple of times but faltered. Finally he grinned and laughed.

"You thought I was Mommy's Boy. You thought *we* was Mommy's Boy. That's smart. That's real smart. You know what? I been killing since I was thirteen. Ain't nobody ever caught me nor pinned anything on me 'cept when I was framed for possession by some asshole narc. And then you come along and say, 'Whoa! This dangerous dude is Mommy's Boy. He's some weird-ass freaky serial killer.' Well, pig, maybe we should show you how we done it."

He glanced down at Campbell, who was staring fixedly at me.

"Now the reverend here, he the blade man. He like to cut. You feel me, cop?"

I spoke, and my voice was thick in my mouth.

"If you hurt her, you'll never get out of here alive."

Campbell spoke for the first time.

"Correction. *If they know* we have hurt her. But we can cut her into little fillets and as long as they think she is unharmed, they will give us what we want." He looked up at Vargas and smiled. "Start calling the press. The bigger the story about these two, the greater the pressure to negotiate."

Vargas looked down at his phone, and Campbell rolled Dehan on her back. He placed his knife at her throat and looked at me. "Drop your gun or I'll cut her throat."

"If you hurt her, they will never give you what you want."

"I'll count to three."

"Don't do this."

Vargas' voice: "*New York Times?* My name is Nelson Vargas. I am Mommy's Boy, and I am holding two NYPD detectives hostage at the Church of the Holy Father and Son at the End of

Days, on Castle Hill Avenue in the Bronx. I wanna tell a reporter about these two detectives. See, they are married..."

Campbell said, "One—"

Vargas said, "But make it quick, bitch, I still have to talk to the networks."

Campbell slipped the knife under Dehan's blouse and cut through the material, exposing her pale belly and her bra. Time seemed to slow down. My eyes swiveled right, and I saw Vargas gloating on the telephone, leering, laughing. They swiveled back to Campbell, slipping the blade of the knife between the cups of the bra, looking at me, shouting, screaming, "*Drop the gun or she dies! I will slice off her breast!*"

And Dehan's silent, screaming eyes, knowing where the blade would go after it cut through her breast.

I bellowed, "*All right! Stop! Stop!*"

And as I hollered the words, I held out the gun in front of me and pulled the trigger twice in rapid succession.

It was a shot at twenty-five feet in a highly stressful situation with a moving target. The risk was high. I could miss and hit Dehan, or I could miss altogether and he would kill her with his knife. But it was the only option open to me. If I had surrendered the gun, we would both have been dead within minutes. So I took the risk, for the three of us.

Both rounds hit home. The first exploded Campbell's left eye, and the second went in just above his jaw, beside his ear, and the back of his head erupted. He half stood and keeled over backward.

I didn't stop to watch. Vargas was gaping at me. I saw the phone drop from his fingers and I was already charging across the room. I reached him as his right arm was emerging from behind his back with his Glock in it. He swung it in a wide arc, and the heavy barrel struck my face, gauging a deep slash across it. The pain was excruciating, and I felt my legs begin to wobble. The gun was coming back for a backhander, which I knew would cost Dehan her life. I could not afford to let it make contact.

Without thinking I smashed my own Sig hard against his wrist as he swung up at my face. He shouted with pain and staggered back. I was unsteady on my feet, and I could hear my breath rasping in my throat. I stepped forward with my left and flung an ineffectual kick with my right at his groin. He staggered back and dropped his weapon, but he was a street fighter, raised in the Bronx, and he wouldn't go down easy.

He clutched at his groin like he'd been hurt badly, and as I closed in, he lunged forward and drove his head into my belly. I was half expecting it and absorbed the blow with my arms, but it threw me off-balance and I stumbled sideways.

Then he came at me, charging, with his fists flying. A powerful right caught me on the shoulder and grazed my head. His left hook connected with my shoulder and my ribs, and a second right hook caught my nose and drove shafts of pain through my head.

He went to raise his weapon again.

Pain can be a great source of power.

Violence, rage, and deep reserves I didn't know I had suddenly welled up inside me, and I stepped close inside his guard with my right foot, blocked his next punch with my left, and put my full two hundred and twenty pounds into a right hook that almost tore off his jaw.

He went down like a sack of wet sand, and I bent unsteadily to remove his shoelaces. I tied his ankles and his wrists behind his back and went to untie Dehan.

NINETEEN

We had stood for a long time, holding each other in that gruesome room, in that dark church. At some point I had pulled my cell from my pocket, and with Dehan clinging to me, I had called the inspector.

"John, what in the name of God!"

His voice had seemed very far away, compared to the soft touch of my wife's hair on my cheek.

"It's over," I had said, softly, as much to Dehan as to the inspector.

A heavy silence, then, "What are you telling me?"

"Dehan is safe, sir . . ." I had had to stop then to fight back the tears. "Dehan is safe, Campbell is dead, and Vargas is bound. Two of Vargas' men are dead downstairs, and two more upstairs. You can send in your men, and the Feds. It's over."

I heard him whisper, "Dear God . . ." again just before I hung up.

Then Dehan looked up into my face. Her eyes were red and swollen and her cheeks were wet. I was about to laugh at her, until she gently wiped the tears from my face. Then I just shut up and held her until we heard the tramping of boots coming up the stairs.

The door burst open, and the SWAT team swarmed in, pointing their weapons at men who were already dead and shouting, "*Clear!*" at each other.

Close behind them came Inspector John Newman, looking pale and drawn, and with him were Agents Panayotes and Trevellian.

The three of them stopped to stare at us a moment. I met Panayotes' eye and gave my head a small shake. To the chief I said, "We'll see you downstairs. Is there an ambulance on its way?"

"Yes, Frank is coming too, and the paramedics . . ."

Trevellian stopped me as we moved toward the door.

"Stone, I'm sorry. I got it badly wrong."

I shook my head again. "Not as much as you think. I need to be with my wife right now. We'll talk."

We made our way down the stairs, past the two grotesque forms on the wooden floor of the lobby, and out onto Castle Hill, where police patrol cars and a SWAT van had already cordoned off the area, and in the distance the howl and wail of approaching sirens clawed the air.

I led Dehan to the ochre wall that enclosed the church, and she leaned against it, wiping her face with her sleeves. I gave her my handkerchief, and she blew her nose noisily. I wiped my own face with my sleeve, and Dehan gave a damp laugh.

"Stone, I am so sorry."

"Don't be stupid."

"I should have been more careful. We know what the Cabras are like. I should have been more careful."

I shook my head. "I should never have let you go."

She batted her eyelashes at me and smiled. "You couldn't have stopped me, big guy," she threw back, and we both laughed. Then she started crying again and had to screw up her face and hold her breath to stop the tears.

"When I think . . ."

"Don't, baby . . ."

She nodded. "Exactly, baby." She clutched her belly with her hands and leaned against me. "When Campbell had the knife . . ."

I couldn't say anything. My jaw was clamped shut too hard. I held her tight and kissed the top of her head.

The growl of an engine and the squeak of tires told me Frank and the ambulances were arriving. I led Dehan out onto the sidewalk, where I corralled Frank and a couple of paramedics. One of them was a black Mother Earth with humorous, compassionate eyes. I handed Dehan over to her.

"She's in shock. She was abducted and her life was threatened. She'll tell you what happened. Look after her." To Frank I said, "Between us, she may be pregnant."

His eyes were two big Os, but Dehan was frowning.

"Where are you going?"

"There is something I have to clear up with the chief. I'll be right back." I looked at Frank. "Keep her with you, Frank, till I get back."

There was a slight narrowing of his eyes, but he nodded. "I will."

I found the chief in the lobby, where they were lifting the bodies onto gurneys. He was on his way out to find me.

"John . . ." He took me aside, holding my shoulder, speaking low with urgent eyes. "John, you can't do this kind of thing."

"Don't ask me to apologize, because I won't."

"There will be an inquiry. You could be suspended. Do you know the risks you took? You could have got both yourself and Dehan killed. And you know full well Vargas' lawyer will start screaming about police brutality and murder. How can we prove you acted in self-defense?"

"I don't care."

His eyebrows shot up. He opened his mouth, but I spoke first.

"They abducted my wife. We just heard she might be pregnant. There were six of them. Two of them jumped me down here, and Campbell was threatening to cut off her breasts and stab her in the womb. Frankly I showed extraordinary restraint, beyond the call of duty, in not killing Vargas when I had the chance. If a jury convicts me on this evidence, then so be it. But I did what I had to do as a man, not a cop, to save my wife and possibly my child. If it's a crime for a man to protect his family, then I'm a criminal. And if it's against the law to save your wife and your child from animals like Campbell and Vargas, then that's a law I am going to break."

"You were *rash* . . ."

"I wasn't rash. The situation called for immediate action." My voice began to rise. "They could have raped, tortured, and murdered her while I exercised a level head!"

"John . . ."

"I'm not going to discuss it, Chief. Do what you have to do. I did what I had to do, and I'll take the consequences and the responsibility."

He sighed and after a moment put a hand on my shoulder. "You know I will stand by you. You were exceptionally courageous, and you cleared up the Mommy's Boy case. That has to count for something."

"Thank you, sir."

"Joe is taking the Kuga away for analysis. We may get lucky. But either way we have Vargas' confession on the phone recorded."

I nodded. "Dehan is in the ambulance with the paramedics . . ."

He frowned at me, like he was seeing me for the first time.

"You look like hell. You're badly bruised and cut. You should be there yourself."

"Yeah, that can keep, sir. There is something I need to do first."

"What, for heaven's sake?"

"I'll call you in a little while."

I made my way back out of the church, shouldering my way through the milling uniforms and the guys in white space suits, crossed Homer Avenue, and found my Jag in the parking lot of the gas station. My whole body was beginning to ache, and I was feeling cold. I knew it was shock, but I had to keep it together a little longer. I fired up the old cat and pulled out onto Castle Hill.

It was a fifteen-minute drive under leaden skies, north along Castle Hill, then west and east along Bronxdale, Bogart, and Pierce until I finally turned left into Hone Avenue and pulled up, after three blocks, outside a tall, narrow redbrick with a stone stoop, seven steps leading to a wooden door protected by a white, wrought iron gate. To the left of the stoop was a garage.

I climbed painfully from the car and made my way up the stairs to ring the bell. Oliver Smith opened the door after a little less than a minute. He smiled under a small frown.

"Detective Stone." His eyes flicked over my shoulder. "You're alone."

"May I come in?"

He hesitated for just a second. "Of course."

He stood back to let me cross the threshold, then closed the door behind me and led the way into a dark living room. The drapes were drawn halfway across the front windows. At the back of the house, light, tinted green by a lawn, filtered through French doors. A dining table and an open-plan kitchen with a breakfast bar stood in shadows. In the living area a sofa and two armchairs in dark, old leather stood grouped around a cold fireplace and a small TV. Most of the walls in the living and dining areas were covered floor to ceiling in books.

An antique folding table stood by the window with chess pieces set out. He seemed to be partway through a game.

I stood looking around, and after a moment I smiled at him.

"The one thing intelligence cannot hide is its own brilliance."

The corner of his mouth twitched, but the frown lingered.

"You're hurt. Oughtn't you see a doctor?"

"That can wait."

"Coffee? A drink?"

I shook my head. "May I sit?"

He gestured at one of the big chairs with both hands. "Please."

I sat, and he took the other one.

"You own and run *Arguably the Best Magazine in Town*."

"Yes, that's true."

I smiled. "That's a very brave title. Long titles are risky, but you pulled it off."

He shrugged. "It's the kind of thing people say in conversation, isn't it? Especially the kind of people who read my magazine. 'Well, it is *arguably* the best magazine in town!' It seems to be catchy."

"I've read it occasionally. It's very good. Intelligent and well informed, without being pretentious. It reminds me of the *New Yorker*, or *Punch*."

"Thank you."

"Your main office is here in New York."

His face had become expressionless. "Yes."

"But I believe you opened another branch in San Francisco. When was that?"

"You know it was five years ago, in June 2015."

"Why do you say I know that, Mr. Smith?"

He spread his hands. "We are not socially acquainted, Detective Stone. So why have you come to visit me?" He pointed at my jacket. "I am guessing you have set your telephone to record and you hope to trick me into saying something which you will frame as incriminating. Mommy's Boy is besting you, and your bosses are pressuring you into getting a result."

I offered him what you might call a bland smile.

"On the contrary." I pointed to my bruised, scarred face. "These were caused by a man who has confessed to being part of a two-man team who were Mommy's Boy. A mad preacher and a barely literate gang member who used the preacher's congregation to select their victims." I gave a small laugh. "The idea that serial killers are charismatic geniuses is a myth perpetuated by Hollywood, but the truth is they are sad, ineffectual men of below-average intelligence who cause a lot of unhappiness, but actually achieve nothing of any value or worth. I came to tell you it was over."

His eyebrows had risen high upon his forehead. There was barely any expression on his face, but what there was was a tiny smile. I knew there was a battle going on inside him, and the euphoria was winning. Finally he could not resist any longer and said, "James Campbell and Nelson Vargas."

"That's remarkable, how did you know that?"

"I have been reading the old case reports. Campbell's mother was the first victim, and James was an early suspect. And I remember a member of the Chupacabras was an early suspect too, Nelson Vargas, but he was eventually eliminated through lack of evidence. It was a small step to put it together from what you told me. Well, then, congratulations are in order."

I screwed up my face. "Mnyah . . ."

"Oh, you're not satisfied."

His face was alive with interest. I shook my head. "Some things just don't quite jibe for me."

"Like?"

"There is no way to connect either Campbell or Vargas with Sharon Lipschitz. They never had any contact."

"Aaahh . . ." He nodded. "The only one who could not be called a whore. A real teaser. I remember wondering, when I read the cases, why did he kill her? She was different from all the rest."

"Exactly. A pattern that had begun to emerge in his killings: the planting of a pattern which was then broken. And what it tells me is that being a whore was never a factor in choosing his victims. He didn't care whether they were whores or not." I sat forward in my chair, shaking my head. "It may well be that over time, if he continues killing, he will even abandon the plump women and the breast cutting. I think all of those features are red herrings. I think there is just one thing that fascinates Mommy's Boy, and that is killing and getting away with it: intellectual vanity."

His face lit up, and he laughed out loud. "You are intelligent, Detective Stone."

"And if that is right, then Campbell and Vargas immediately lose credibility as suspects. Because to them, as misogynists, it is those very qualities: the fact of the women being whores in their eyes, the plump, maternal bodies, the breasts, the womb—all of these are core factors for these two men. Intellectual vanity is barely an issue for Campbell; it is nonexistent for Vargas. They were set up in a frame by the real Mommy's Boy, who is not a mommy's boy at all."

"He's not? I imagine the FBI have profiled him. Those guys are pretty good at that kind of thing."

"A profiler is only as good as his data."

"True. So what other data did you have to work with? He must have given some clue to his character. Though if he is a true genius, like Shakespeare, he might leave no trace of his own personality in his work."

"His work?"

"Undoubtedly that is how he sees it."

"Perhaps. I think it is more a punishment killing."

He frowned. "Punishment for what?"

"Betrayal." He shrugged, shook his head. I went on. "He kids himself into believing that it's all about intellectual vanity, besting the cops and the system. He probably sees himself as an intellectual anarchist, defying the system at every turn and defeating it. I figure he has had to survive for decades without the support of a mother or a father, depending on his intelligence . . ."

"Aren't you contradicting yourself? I thought you said he was of average intelligence or below."

I shook my head. "No. Serial killers on the whole are below average, but this guy *is* smart. Not as smart as he thinks, but he is smart. And he has had to rely on his intelligence since he was thirteen . . ."

"Thirteen? That is very precise."

"Yeah, that's the age he was when his mother was murdered.

He didn't know his father, because his mother was a prostitute. So you see, to pretend to himself that the nature of the murders has no connection to his emotional baggage is to be in denial. He is very clever at subverting it and using it to confuse the cops, but the fact is he kills these women to punish his mother."

"Punish her for what, for heaven's sake? It was not her fault she got murdered!"

"Oh, but it was. Alaska has the highest incidence of serial killings in the USA, possibly the world, because serial killers go there to hunt. There are a lot of prostitutes servicing the seasonal labor, and his mother was one of them. And it was by being a prostitute that she got killed, and he watched it. She betrayed him and abandoned him, as he had always known she would, as she did every night when she took a client to her bed, and he had to lie there in his room listening to yet another man grunt and fumble over his mother. And finally, that night, which must feel like an eternal nightmare in his memory, she was killed and she went away, abandoned him forever: irrecoverable."

His face was like gray marble. His eyes were dead, his mouth expressionless.

"My, that's quite a creation."

"I checked with the DMV." He went rigid. I went on. "You do indeed own an MG MGB from 1969..."

"Well, that's what I told you..."

"But you also own a 2014 Ford Kuga, in off-white." I told him the license plate and added, "And you were caught on the CCTV at the gas station around the corner from Claire Carter's house on the day she was killed, driving that very car."

He shook his head. "No, that day I was at home, and that car was in a lockup. You cannot possibly have seen me in the CCTV footage..."

"Why? Because you were dressed as a woman on the way there? Because you were disguised on the way back?" I laughed. "That car was at Claire Carter's house, Mr. Smith, and I would like to know how it came to be there. I would also like to know how come you saw it and you didn't recognize it as your own."

He was laughing, but it was a strained laugh, and his face was flushed. "No, no, Detective. You don't understand. I bought that car a long time ago and I never use it. I always use the MG. I haven't seen that car in years. It's been in a lockup!"

I made the face of understanding and nodded. "Oh, I see. When did you buy it?"

"Oh." He flapped a hand. "Back in the day, when I lived in New York before."

"Before you moved to San Francisco, to set up the other office . . ."

"Exactly."

"Back in May of 2015 . . ."

"Yes, oh, five years ago. That's why the car was in the lockup."

"One month after the murders stopped here in New York."

He shrugged, stammered, laughed. "Hardly evidence of murder, Detective."

"One month before the murders started in San Francisco."

"Did they? I wasn't aware."

I lied then. "The car is being recovered right now from the lockup."

He froze. "What? No. How could you possibly know where the lockup is?"

"It's called diligent police work. There was a BOLO out for it, and local cops have been making inquiries. A witness told us a Kuga fitting that description was being kept in a lockup nearby. He thought it was strange it was never used, but the other day it was taken out and put back in the space of a few hours. Now, if you didn't take it out and put it back, who did?"

"How could I possibly know? I haven't been near the place in years."

"And then there is the forensics, modern face recognition of the gas station footage, and the analysis of the products inside the car."

"Face recognition?"

"Yeah, once the image is cleaned up, we can match the face on the footage inside the store to your face with a ninety-eight percent accuracy."

He said, "No . . ." Then he frowned and his eyes narrowed. "What products?"

"The makeup and the essential oil. They'll be able to date the residues. You did transport the makeup in that car, didn't you? And the oil."

"Makeup . . ."

I made a deliberate mistake. "Lancome—"

His brows knit, he whispered, "L'Oréal."

"And tea tree oil—"

"Lavender . . ."

"Your mother used L'Oréal."

He nodded. "And she was one of those pseudo-aromatherapists, always using lavender oil for everything. If you scratched your finger, lavender oil, if you grazed your knee—heaven forbid you ever did!—lavender oil! If you sneezed, lavender oil! She *destroyed* her son, murdered him, while he tried to sleep listening to her flirting and laughing and humping every lumberjack in two hundred miles square. You can't use lavender oil to cure those wounds. She put lavender oil on my cuts and bruises to salve the damage to my body, but she left my heart and my soul gaping and suppurating."

"I made inquiries. Your mother was murdered, and you witnessed it."

"Dear God, how I hated that woman. And when I watched her strangled and stabbed by that animal, I felt nothing but liberation, and I wanted more than anything else to be like him."

"He was caught, tried, and convicted."

"Yes, he was deeply stupid. I spent years thinking about that night and the thousand and one ways he could have avoided being caught. I also thought about what I could have done, with my intellect, if my mother had supported me and helped me instead of sentencing me to the life of a whore's son in remote Alaska. In the end . . ." He shrugged, then simpered. "It was too tempting not to give it a try. I drove down to the great urban jungle of Los Angeles. I had thoroughly researched the forensic methods and capabilities of the LAPD, and I selected a random prostitute in Watts. I killed her, left no trace of myself, and kept tabs on the news over the next month. You wouldn't believe the lack of interest that killing generated."

He sighed. "The killing itself was enjoyable, like your first fuck with a girl who is available but not your type. So I began to practice with different girls in different places. I guess Freud was right and we all ultimately seek our mother, because I have to tell you I got a *huge* kick out of killing my first fat, jolly woman. It was the most intense sexual pleasure I had ever experienced. And that is what I have stuck to ever since."

I prompted him. "But in the end it was not intellectually satisfying . . ."

"No. Not at all. It was like being married to a stupid woman. You begin to *hunger* for the intellectual stimulus. It's not enough to fuck, you need the conversation too. So I set up a game of chess with your PD. And I may say they were very sadly lacking. Alvarez was a total ass. You, I have to hand it to you, were quite brilliant. I should never have gone to see you, that was a big mistake; never told you about the car. I thought that would send you off on a wild goose chase, or a wild Kuga chase, but it didn't. I should never have gone," he repeated, "but I couldn't resist the curiosity."

I gestured at him. "You are the gray man. You are largely nondescript, and if I am not mistaken, your mother smothered you, didn't she? She was overprotective, overmothering, cosseted you . . ."

His face darkened. "She tried to turn me into a little girl, forever sprinkling me with that damned lavender, dressing me in cute little clothes, pouring damned cologne in my hair and slicking it down." His voice became a growl. "She smothered me with her breasts and erased every trace of masculinity from me. For which I suppose I should thank her . . ."

I nodded. "Because you were able to gain access to these women's houses by dressing as a woman. You have a light, almost feminine voice, learnt from her, I guess."

"Yes." He gave a short, dry laugh. "Women have this crazy idea that men are dangerous and women are not. They will *always* open the door to a girl. The number of women I have killed because they were willing to open the door to another woman! They don't realize that *women* are the killers of the race, not men!"

I reached in my pocket and pulled out my cell. I laid it on the table so he could see it was recording. Then I switched it off.

"You know what happens now?"

He nodded. "You Mirandize me."

"You'll be tried and then you'll be taken to a supermax prison, for the rest of your life. You will spend weeks on end in solitary confinement, and the few people you have contact with won't be up to your intellectual bootlaces. You will probably never again have an intelligent conversation, as long as you live."

He blinked, vaguely astonished, and I went on.

"And then there's what those inmates do to pedophiles and serial killers, especially men like you, who are delicate, feminine, and sensitive." I could feel a cold, ruthless hardness inside me, like ancient ice congealing. "They will rape you and beat you, every day, and the wardens won't even allow you to commit suicide. In some supermax prisons, the staff are worse than the inmates. You will pay for what you have done, with interest, every day of your life."

"Oh . . ."

"Do you own a gun?"

"Yes."

We sat for a long while, staring at each other. Finally I said, "Oliver Smith, I am putting you under arrest for the murder of Claire Carter and other women. You have the right to remain silent. Anything you say can and will be used against you in a court of law. You have the right to a lawyer before we ask you any questions and during questioning. If you cannot afford a lawyer, one will be appointed for you. If you decide to answer questions now without a lawyer present, you have the right to change your mind at any time. Do you understand me?"

"Yes."

"Then you'd better go get a bag and pack it. I'm taking you downtown, and you won't be coming back."

"I need to go upstairs."

I followed him up and waited outside his room while he went inside. I wasn't surprised when he emerged a couple of minutes later holding a .38 revolver. He looked pale and sick. Maybe he'd never killed a man before. He raised the weapon and pointed it at me, and it was dancing in his shaking hands. He said:

"I tried to do it, but I can't. You'll have to do it for me."

"And save you the suffering? Your due punishment? Why should I?"

"Because I'll kill you if you don't."

"You? You kill women. You haven't got the balls to kill a man."

His face turned ugly. There was viciousness and a rage in his eyes, and suddenly I saw the man who killed the women. His voice became an ugly hiss, his neck corded with tendons.

"You think I won't? You think I can't? I'll blow your fucking knees off and then I'll go looking for *your fucking wife*! *And you can live the rest of your fucking life knowing what I did to her!*"

He ended in a scream, his face flushed with rage. I acknowledged to myself later that it was what I had hoped for. In the moment I was justified, and I didn't think. A wild fury welled up inside me, and I snatched the barrel of the gun with my left hand

and levered it back, in toward him, and with my right I squeezed his finger, where it lay still on the trigger. The .38 exploded, and at point-blank range the slug tore through his face and into his head. His body jerked and flailed for a second or two and then fell to the carpeted floor with a big, ugly thud.

EPILOGUE

She was lying on the sofa, with a duvet over her and a mug of cocoa in her hands the size of a milk churn. The fire was crackling, and the flames were dancing in the dusky windows. I had not yet closed the drapes, and the houses across the road were the pale gray-blue ghosts of homes, where one by one warm, amber windows were giving them life.

"You realize, Stone," she said, "that I am exploiting you. I don't need this mollycoddling, but I am enjoying it. You went through as much as I did..."

"No, I didn't, and I am not pregnant."

"How did you know it was Smith, Stone? It never even crossed my mind."

I shrugged and sighed with the bottle of Bushmills halfway to my glass.

"It became obvious when we started looking into Sharon Lipschitz that it could not be Campbell and Vargas, but it also became clear that they were being partially framed. Not as a serious frame, but as a hint, a taunt, part of a game of cat and mouse, where he pushed us one way and then another.

"Trevellian's profile made me think too. It was obvious to me that our killer's tactics were working even with the profiler. He was painting a picture of himself that was misleading. At the same time, I got the feeling that Trevellian *was* seeing something of the real Mommy's Boy, but, as I had felt from the start, it was like two people, both inhabiting the same person, almost like a split personality. On the exterior was the agreeable, helpful, highly intelligent Oliver Smith, but hidden inside was the twisted, tortured, psychotic killer. I got a brief glimpse of him just before I shot him."

I sighed and went on. "Then there was the recurring description of the man who emerged from Claire Carter's house as being nondescript, and when I pushed Edna Brown about him, she wasn't even sure if he was black or white. That suggested to me an answer to a question I'd had from the start. How was this guy getting into the houses? He might have been a client of some of the women, but, as always, that didn't wash with Sharon Lipschitz.

"But if he was posing as a woman, and carrying it off, then they would be far more inclined to let him in if he provided a reasonable excuse. I asked Edna if she had seen a woman, earlier in the day, and she said she had.

"That got me thinking, because I had noticed from the start that there was something feminine, if not effeminate, about Smith. It was a hunch more than anything else. The fact that he had just happened to be there, and came forward. So I did a check to see what car he owned, and he owned two: a classic MG and an old-model Ford Kuga. That was too much of a coincidence."

She made a face like mental constipation. "What *was* the whole thing with the Kuga? I don't see the point in that."

I nodded and smiled. "Yeah, that was kind of the point. His way of doing things was to spread confusion. He had an old Ford Kuga, from years back, and he thought that if he used it for the killing and then stuck it back in his lockup, we would go off looking for someone with a white Ford SUV and ignore him because he had a classic MG. What he never expected was that we would look at it the other way and inquire as to what other cars he had. It's the same thinking that had him set up the patterns and then break them. It almost worked."

She frowned, grunted, and shook her head. "So, why did Vargas confess to it?"

I gave a small laugh. "It played right into his hands. His snatching you had been opportunistic. His first plan was much more desperado. He aimed to try and kill Panayotes' team, or Jose, or both. But when he saw you on the sidewalk, he seized on a better plan. To use you as a hostage. And then, obviously, the more public sympathy he could drum up for you and me, the more pressure he could put on the mayor and the police department to play ball. Likewise, the more terrible he could make himself seem, the more of a threat to you, the more pressure the public would put on the authorities to abide by his terms."

We were quiet for a while. She sipping her hot chocolate, and me allowing the golden water of life to ease my painful body. I sat and lifted her legs onto mine, and we sat watching each other for a while. Finally she said, "Kate phoned."

I felt a hot pellet in my gut, of both fear and pleasure. A thousand questions crowded my mind about what our future would now be. Too many questions. All I could do was stare at her like an idiot and say, "Oh . . ."

A tear rolled along her lower lid, and she gave a small shrug. The smile was a sad one.

"False alarm," she said. "Just a false alarm."

"Oh."

Don't miss BLEED OUT. The riveting sequel in the Dead Cold Mystery series.

Scan the QR code below to purchase BLEED OUT.

Or go to: righthouse.com/bleed-out

NOTE: flip to the very end to read an exclusive sneak peak...

DON'T MISS ANYTHING!

If you want to stay up to date on all new releases in this series, with this author, or with any of our new deals, you can do so by joining our newsletters below.

In addition, you will immediately gain access to our entire *Right House VIP Library*, which includes many riveting Mystery and Thriller novels for your enjoyment!

righthouse.com/email

(Easy to unsubscribe. No spam. Ever.)

ALSO BY BLAKE BANNER

Up to date books can be found at:
www.righthouse.com/blake-banner

ROGUE THRILLERS
Gates of Hell (Book 1)
Hell's Fury (Book 2)

ALEX MASON THRILLERS
Odin (Book 1)
Ice Cold Spy (Book 2)
Mason's Law (Book 3)
Assets and Liabilities (Book 4)
Russian Roulette (Book 5)
Executive Order (Book 6)
Dead Man Talking (Book 7)
All The King's Men (Book 8)
Flashpoint (Book 9)
Brotherhood of the Goat (Book 10)
Dead Hot (Book 11)
Blood on Megiddo (Book 12)
Son of Hell (Book 13)

HARRY BAUER THRILLER SERIES
Dead of Night (Book 1)
Dying Breath (Book 2)
The Einstaat Brief (Book 3)
Quantum Kill (Book 4)
Immortal Hate (Book 5)
The Silent Blade (Book 6)
LA: Wild Justice (Book 7)

Breath of Hell (Book 8)
Invisible Evil (Book 9)
The Shadow of Ukupacha (Book 10)
Sweet Razor Cut (Book 11)
Blood of the Innocent (Book 12)
Blood on Balthazar (Book 13)
Simple Kill (Book 14)
Riding The Devil (Book 15)
The Unavenged (Book 16)
The Devil's Vengeance (Book 17)
Bloody Retribution (Book 18)
Rogue Kill (Book 19)
Blood for Blood (Book 20)

DEAD COLD MYSTERY SERIES
An Ace and a Pair (Book 1)
Two Bare Arms (Book 2)
Garden of the Damned (Book 3)
Let Us Prey (Book 4)
The Sins of the Father (Book 5)
Strange and Sinister Path (Book 6)
The Heart to Kill (Book 7)
Unnatural Murder (Book 8)
Fire from Heaven (Book 9)
To Kill Upon A Kiss (Book 10)
Murder Most Scottish (Book 11)
The Butcher of Whitechapel (Book 12)
Little Dead Riding Hood (Book 13)
Trick or Treat (Book 14)
Blood Into Wine (Book 15)
Jack In The Box (Book 16)
The Fall Moon (Book 17)
Blood In Babylon (Book 18)
Death In Dexter (Book 19)
Mustang Sally (Book 20)

A Christmas Killing (Book 21)
Mommy's Little Killer (Book 22)
Bleed Out (Book 23)
Dead and Buried (Book 24)
In Hot Blood (Book 25)
Fallen Angels (Book 26)
Knife Edge (Book 27)
Along Came A Spider (Book 28)
Cold Blood (Book 29)
Curtain Call (Book 30)

THE OMEGA SERIES
Dawn of the Hunter (Book 1)
Double Edged Blade (Book 2)
The Storm (Book 3)
The Hand of War (Book 4)
A Harvest of Blood (Book 5)
To Rule in Hell (Book 6)
Kill: One (Book 7)
Powder Burn (Book 8)
Kill: Two (Book 9)
Unleashed (Book 10)
The Omicron Kill (Book 11)
9mm Justice (Book 12)
Kill: Four (Book 13)
Death In Freedom (Book 14)
Endgame (Book 15)

ABOUT US

Right House is an independent publisher created by authors for readers. We specialize in Action, Thriller, Mystery, and Crime novels.

If you enjoyed this novel, then there is a good chance you will like what else we have to offer! Please stay up to date by using any of the links below.

Join our mailing lists to stay up to date -->
righthouse.com/email
Visit our website --> righthouse.com
Contact us --> contact@righthouse.com

facebook.com/righthousebooks
x.com/righthousebooks
instagram.com/righthousebooks

EXCLUSIVE SNEAK PEAK OF...

BLEED OUT

CHAPTER 1

"I've been interested in this one for a while," I said, and looked across at her. She had both elbows on her desk, which abutted mine, and her cheeks squashed between her fists as she stared at the screen of her computer.

"Uh-huh . . ."

I waited. Eventually the silence encroached on her, as it was meant to, and she shifted her gaze to frown at me.

"What?"

I waved the file at her. "I am going to tell you from the beginning, so be patient and listen."

She sighed and flopped back in her chair. I said, "Sadie Byrne, nineteen years of age . . ."

"How long ago?"

"Fall of 2018, late September, listen. Try not to talk." She sighed again and crossed her arms. I went on. "Okay, so Sadie Byrne starts to become depressed . . ."

"Being nineteen will do that to you."

"Be quiet, Dehan. She starts to become depressed. So much so that her parents eventually take her to the doctor, who refers them to a psychiatrist. After a few visits, when Dad goes to collect her—"

"From the shrink?"

"Yes, from the psychiatrist, Dad goes to collect her and . . ." I scanned the page for the name. "Dr. Shaw asks him to come into her office with Sadie. It turns out she has been raped."

Dehan winced. "How long before?"

"About four months prior, though she refuses to state an exact date. Thing is, she also refuses to name her rapist, or even specify how or where it happened." Dehan interjected a skeptical grunt. "Meanwhile, Dr. Shaw, who seems to be no slouch, noticed that Sadie was not looking too healthy. It might be her depression, or it might be something else. So she sends her for blood tests."

"Dr. Shaw is a woman, right?"

I glanced at her. "Yeah. Why?"

She shrugged. "She's intuitive. So she sent her for blood tests, what happened? She was pregnant?"

I shook my head. "No, she was HIV positive, and it had developed into AIDS."

She sat forward, and her eyebrows arched. "In *four months*?"

"Yeah. A very small percentage of people are termed rapid progressors, and in extreme cases can develop from contracting the virus to death in as little as a year. This was Sadie's case. A combination of poor diet, depression, lack of exercise, and a refusal to take antiretroviral medication meant she died roughly a year after her alleged rape."

She was frowning at me. "But you know that doesn't constitute murder, right? Knowingly infecting somebody with HIV is a misdemeanor in New York. In Iowa I think they take 'em out and shoot 'em like dawgs, but here in civilized New York it's a misdemeanor, unless you can prove cruel intent and a depraved state of mind. I forget the exact wording."

I nodded patiently. "I know . . ."

"And rape? We have never investigated a rape *per se*. We've always looked at homicides. Rape is *real* hard to prove as a cold case, Stone. Especially if the victim is dead *and* didn't report it at the time. How long did you say? Four months!"

"You done?"

"Yeah."

"Then sit back and listen, like I told you from the start."

"Okay." She sat back and laced her fingers over her belly.

"The curious thing is that this case cross-references to another case."

"What case?"

"Chuck Inglewood..."

"Rings a bell. Stabbed to death? Weird circumstances?"

"If you'll stop talking, Motor Mouth, I'll tell you. His wife, Angela Inglewood, was visiting with neighbors in the afternoon. Chuck, who was apparently not great at socializing, stayed home. According to Angela, as he was at home and it was afternoon, she left the French windows open, presumably onto the backyard. While she was having coffee with her neighbor, one Violet Nowak, she heard her phone ringing, but it stopped before she could answer it. She checked and saw that Chuck had tried to call her a total of six times. She tried calling him back but without success. The number was engaged. So she made her apologies, collected her things, and hurried home, about a hundred yards or so down the road.

"She entered the house, called him, got no answer, and eventually found him upstairs in their bedroom. He had been savagely attacked, cut with a knife, very deep wounds in his underarms and the insides of his thighs. He had bled profusely. His cell was in his right hand, and he had apparently called 911 because the cops and an ambulance showed up a minute or two later."

She had been nodding while I spoke. Now she said, "Yeah, I remember. Who had that case? Reynolds?"

"Reynolds and Hogben."

"That was a weird case. Absolutely zero forensics, no motive... So how does it cross-reference to Sadie Byrne?"

I shrugged. "When I say it cross-references, what I really mean is that I have found a connection. Nobody else has until now. Only me."

"Hey, Stone." She said it in a flat monotone. "You're brilliant. You know, maybe I don't tell you often enough. You're brilliant, Stone, you're brilliant . . ." Mo, across the aisle, groaned. She ignored him. "So how are they connected?"

"Chuck Inglewood was Sadie Byrne's uncle by marriage."

"Holy cow . . ."

"See? I told you. It's interesting. Cathy Byrne, Sadie's mother, was Angela Inglewood's sister."

"Are we seeing a hint of a motive here?"

I dropped the file on the desk and spread my hands. "That Chuck raped his niece and either Patrick or Cathy Byrne found out and went around and killed him? It's possible, but at this stage there is zero evidence to support such a theory."

She stuck out her lower lip and nodded. "Then again, somebody wanted to kill him. If they wanted to kill him, they had a motive. No motive was ever established, and yet . . ."

"We'll put it in the possible pile."

"Okay, so let's go see what else we can find. Where do you want to start?"

I pointed at her computer. "While you were staring at the screen of your diabolical machine, I called Angela Inglewood and asked if we could go and see the house. She said she didn't live there anymore. She'd moved out almost immediately after the murder, locked the place up, stayed a couple of months with her sister, and then bought a house in Throggs Neck."

"Huh . . ."

"But she said if we want to, we can collect the key from Mrs. Nowak and have a look around."

She nodded for a bit. "What was I doing?"

"Staring at your computer screen. It's an affliction that affects some people your age."

I stood and grabbed my jacket. She watched me and said, "What? Sorry. I was staring at my screen and I didn't hear you."

As we passed Mo on the way out he muttered under his

breath, "Jaysus! Curdle a guy's breakfast. Don't hurry back, will ya?"

It was a warm afternoon. The leaves on the plane trees on Story Avenue were still young and fresh and green, but the sky was losing that freshly washed look that belonged to March and April and had acquired that fresh, sun-and-wind-dried look that belonged to May and June.

We climbed into my ancient, burgundy Jaguar, rolled down the windows, and fired up the big engine. The cat growled its way down to White Plains Road, with the wind whipping Dehan's hair across her face, and we turned left and north to pass over the Bruckner Expressway. Along the way, Dehan shook her head and drummed her fingers on the open window. Finally she held out her hand, palm up, like Hamlet holding up Yorick's skull.

"She leaves the house, she locks it up and never goes back, she moves to Throggs Neck and buys a *new* house, but she never sells the old one."

I made a slow shrug. "Never . . . We're talking about maybe eighteen months."

She grunted. "Did she put it on the market?"

"I don't know yet. What are you driving at?"

"I don't know." She raised her open right hand again, like she really wanted me to look at Yorick's skull. "This is an odd case, so I am trying to question the things that seem most odd. And it seems odd to me that she would just walk away from the house and buy a new one, without trying to sell the old one."

"That's true." I glanced at her. "But it's not, on the face of it, the behavior of someone who is trying to conceal evidence."

She stared at me without expression, nodded, and looked out of the window. "No," she said. "It's not."

I turned right onto Virginia, and then right again onto Haviland, and stopped outside a large, two-story house set back from the road among its own lawns, with an independent double garage in back. The lawns were overgrown, and what had once been flower beds bordering the house were now more like neglected burial mounds for very small people. I climbed out of the car and walked around to rest against the far side of the car, looking up the concrete driveway toward the double garage. Dehan came and stood next to me.

"They weren't poor. What did he do?"

"He was a plumber. That's to say, he had a plumbing business. Employed a handful of guys and ran a plumbing supplies shop."

She nodded sagely. "People joke about it, but it's true. Lawyers, dentists, and plumbers."

I pointed along the drive. "Unusual."

"What is?"

"People usually have their French windows in back, so you can open them onto the lawn. This guy has his at the side of the house, leading onto a concrete driveway and his garage."

She took in what I was saying, gazing up the drive, then stared at me. "Is that significant?"

"I don't know. We'll see. It's visible from the road. If it was open, anyone passing would see it. And just over there . . ." I pointed past the double garage, at the backs of the houses that ran parallel along Powell Avenue. ". . . is where Sadie Byrne lived."

"Huh . . . pretty close. Almost visible from the top floor."

"Let's go get the keys."

We strolled down the street, among the mottled shade of the chestnut trees, listening to the raucous chatter of the starlings above in the green leaves, and the boisterous laughter of the kids in the playground opposite the houses. After we'd passed a few standalones, we came to a cute terrace of gabled redbricks, each with a flight of nine steps leading up to a porch set over a garage. The first was Mrs. Nowak's, and I climbed up to ring on the doorbell.

The door opened, and I had to look down to see her. She was four foot eleven and had hair the color of ripe tomatoes. A few strands of brown hair protruded from her upper lip, as though somebody had put them there by mistake. She studied my face with shrewd eyes, and then gave Dehan the same treatment.

"What?"

I showed her my badge. "NYPD. I'm Detective Stone; this is Detective Dehan. Are you Mrs. Nowak?"

"What if I yam?" Her voice was rapid and nasal.

"I believe Mrs. Inglewood has been in touch with you about the keys . . . ?"

"Don't come in! You not allowed to come in without a warrant! Stay there, on the stoop!"

She went away, into the shadows of the house, all knees and elbows and slippers. Desultory sounds: grunts, soft curses, and mild blasphemy wafted out to us, followed shortly by Mrs. Nowak holding a small key ring with a number of keys on it. She handed them to me, then yanked them back as I reached for them.

"You bring 'em back! They not mine, see! I ain't been in the-ya. I ain't touched nothin'! She gave 'em to me on trust. And I have to give 'em back to her when she sells the goddamn place. If she ever does!"

"We'll bring them right back."

"Cops, ain'tcha?" She slapped the keys in my hand, muttered something that sounded vile about "goddamn cops," and closed the door.

We made our way back down the steps. Dehan muttered, "And Angela Inglewood spent a couple of hours with that woman? Why would you do that?"

"Perhaps she was nicer back then."

She shook her head. "Uh-uh. It takes years to get like that. It's a process, like erosion, or developing a bunion."

We came to the Inglewoods' house. Dehan made for the front door, but I went 'round the side to have a look at the French windows. The drapes were drawn inside. I went and touched the doors, tried the handle. It felt solid. Dehan came 'round the corner to watch me, then joined me as I made my way to the rear of the house.

"Something's on your mind," she said. "I can tell."

"If it's not now," I said cryptically, "it will be soon."

She nodded. "Oh, should I hit you now, or wait till we get inside?"

"I'm just wondering how the killer got in."

We had got to the back of the house, and there was another door there. This one was a normal wooden door with a square pane of glass at the top that was reinforced with a kind of chicken-wire mesh inside it. It had two locks beneath an old-fashioned lever handle. One was Chubb, the other Yale. I pointed at the door.

"You reckon that door has a couple of dead bolts on the inside?"

"Yeah, I do, but you've clearly been thinking about this case for a while, Stone, and have formed some opinions already. Didn't you tell me the killer got in through the French windows?"

I nodded, stepping across the overgrown lawn to the far side of the house. "Yes. Well, what I in fact said was that Angela Inglewood said that she had gone to Mrs. Nowak's and left the French windows open."

She came after me, taking long strides. "So isn't that the obvious way in? Especially as it's visible from the road!"

I was surprised by the comment and showed her my surprise with my face. She grunted, "No, okay, you're right. Of course, seeing the door from the road and slipping in would suggest an opportunistic killing, and this killing was not in any way opportunistic. But still, I mean, if the doors were open . . ."

I nodded and made my way back to the front of the house, speaking over my shoulder. "That is important, very important."

I came to the front door, pulling out the key from my pocket. Dehan followed slowly, watching her feet. "So maybe he'd been watching, casing the joint, waiting for an opportunity."

"That's possible."

"Somebody with a grudge . . ."

"Definitely."

"Who had been watching and waiting, and when Angela went out, he saw the door open and seized the opportunity."

I unlocked the door, pushed, and stepped inside.

The first impression was the unpleasant, fetid smell on the air. The place was in shadow, with only occasional shafts of dusty light piercing the gloom. It took a moment for my eyes to adjust, and then I saw that we were stepping into a very large space that stretched out on either side of the front door. There was no fireplace, and the room had more the feel of a lounge in a hotel or an airport than a living room. There was a huge white leather sofa in the middle of the floor, with two vast, overstuffed white leather armchairs opposite, and in the middle a white wrought iron, glass, and brass coffee table. On one wall, to the left as we came in, there was a TV the size of a small cinema screen, with four independent speakers dotted about the room. So you could evade the real world and make the fake world seem as real as the one you were escaping from.

There was a flight of stairs at the back, rising in a dogleg to what I figured was an attic space above. A door beside the stairs led to the back of the house. I guessed there would be a kitchen and a bathroom. And over on the right, with the drapes drawn across them, were the French windows, which had stood open and admitted Chuck Inglewood's killer, eighteen months ago. Dehan spoke, pointing at the drapes, where the dusty light filtered in like a weak halo around the dark oblong.

"He came in there. He crossed the room to the stairs . . ."

"Wooden stairs."

"Is that important?"

"They creak."

"Oh, okay, yeah, obviously. So, he crossed to the wooden stairs, he climbed them to the bedroom . . ." She paused. "So he must have been quick. Real quick. As you say, Chuck would have heard him, so he had to get up there before Chuck reacted." She paused, staring up at the top of the steps. "And in the bedroom he attacked him and killed him." She stared at me. "He must have known the house, and he must have known what he was going to find here."

I nodded and sighed. "Yes, let's go upstairs."

She led the way, and they creaked.

CHAPTER 2

The stairs, which were noisy, went up through a hole in the ceiling to a floor where it was even gloomier than down below, and the rancid smell was worse. The landing was horseshoe-shaped, carpeted wall-to-wall in cream, with a door on the left and another opposite on the right. Dehan paused on the last step, glanced at the door on the left, and said, "That's got to be a john."

I watched her step up, open the door, and lean in; dim light filtered out across her face and her hair. "No," she said. "It's not a john. It's an office."

I went and stood beside her. It was a long, oblong room with panoramic windows overlooking the backyard and, over the rooftops, Powell Avenue, where the Byrnes lived. On the far right there was a two-seater sofa, an armchair, and a coffee table, and, running the length of the room under the window, he had a long desk. There were files and papers, mostly orders and tax returns, invoices and bills. A bank of plug sockets had been screwed to the wall, just below the windowsill. I pointed at it.

"I wonder where the computer is."

"Maybe they took it to the lab."

I shook my head. "Nothing about that in the file. We should ask."

I stepped out of the office and crossed the landing to the door opposite. The foul smell grew stronger as I approached. I heard Dehan swear behind me and glanced over my shoulder as I took hold of the handle.

"I don't think this place has been cleaned since he was killed."

She had her hand over her nose and mouth and nodded. Her voice came out muffled. "She just closed up the house and walked away."

I pushed open the door. The stench made me back away, fighting down the reflex to retch. Dehan swore again, turned, and walked to the banisters. "*Puta chingada!* Holy . . . ! Sweet mother of Jesus!" She turned and stared at me. "They took the body, right?"

I nodded. "But they didn't take the sheets."

I pulled the handkerchief from my pocket and covered my nose and mouth, then pushed through the door again. There was a window opposite the door, and another over on the left, overlooking the drive. Both were shut and both had the drapes closed, with only hazy light filtering around the sides. The bed was large, probably six foot six square, and it was swarming with flies. The duvet was roughly in place, as though the bed had recently been made and then rumpled slightly. In the half-light, it looked like the bedding was dark brown, or even black, but then I noticed that the rug on which the bed was standing, which should have been cream, was also dark.

Dehan spoke through the crook of her arm, which was covering her nose and mouth.

"She just walked away . . . She left the bed, with all his blood . . ."

"That smell isn't the blood, Dehan, not after eighteen months."

She glanced at me over her arm. ". . . rats."

I looked around. On my left, across the polished wood floor, a door stood half-open onto a tiled en suite bathroom that was in deep shadows. I crossed the room, pulled back the drapes, and opened the window. Dehan did the same at the other end of the room. Air and bright sunlight streamed in and flooded the room and the bed. There was a flurry of rustles and scrabbling, and a rat darted from under the bed and scuttled into the en suite.

"We'll have to get pest control in here. Look..."

On the far side, away from the door, the carpet, the duvet, and parts of the mattress, where they had been saturated with blood, had been chewed, eaten away. Dehan hunkered down and peered under the bed. Her nose wrinkled and her nostrils dilated.

"There are holes in the wall. They've chewed right through, but there are..." She paused while she counted. "At least six dead rats here, and a couple of plastic trays."

She stood, pulled her cell from her pocket, and made the call. While she was doing that, I went into the bathroom. There was a tube of toothpaste on the sink, two toothbrushes in a glass. In the cabinet there was a bottle of painkillers, a couple of disposable razors, a box of tampons, floss. A tall cabinet against the wall, beside the bathtub, held towels and toilet rolls. Behind the shower curtain, at the end of the bath, I found shampoo, shower gel, a pink disposable razor.

When I returned to the bedroom, I found Dehan, with her hands on her hips, standing at the top of the stairs, staring down over the banisters.

"So what happened here, Stone?" She began to move down the stairs as she spoke. "It's early afternoon. We don't know where he is. Maybe he's in his office, working. Maybe he's in the kitchen, clearing up after lunch. Whatever..."

She had reached the bottom of the stairs and was looking around the living room. I stood beside her, trying to visualize the scene.

"She goes to him, or she calls to him, 'I'm going down the road to visit with Mrs. Nowak.'"

She pointed across the room to the drapes, then walked over

and pulled them back. The midday sun glared in. She held out her hands to me, and I tossed her the keys. She unlocked the glass doors and slid them back so that fresh, bright air entered the room.

"These doors are open," she said. "So, in all probability, she leaves through here, right? Or does she go to the front door? It doesn't matter, either way, she leaves. She goes out and down to the sidewalk, she turns right and walks for a minute or less, climbs the stairs to the stoop, and goes in to have coffee."

She stopped, and I took over. "And we assume that Chuck's killer, who is nearby, sees her do that. Meanwhile, wherever he is, and whatever he is doing, Chuck winds up going upstairs to the bedroom. What made him do that? If the bathroom is as they left it, like the rest of the house, there are no towels waiting to be washed, no clothes on the floor, no indication that he had just had a bath or a shower. Also, his body was dressed. So maybe he went up to work, but then why is he in the bedroom? What made him go to the bedroom?"

She was facing me, silhouetted against the bright sunlight. There was now a faint smell of sweet roses on the air.

"Okay, let's park that to one side for now. We know he wound up upstairs because that's where his body was found and that's where all his blood was. What made him go up there, we don't know, for now. But for the sake of the argument, let's say he was in his office; Angela had gone, so there is nobody downstairs. The killer sees her leave and sees the French doors are open. So he comes in. Here it gets tricky . . ."

I walked past her and stepped out onto the broad, concrete drive. The day was growing warm. I glanced over to the shade of the plane trees that fringed the road. Dehan was in the doorway behind me, leaning on the jamb. I said:

"Okay, backtrack a minute. On the face of it we have two options: one, that the killer was passing and happened to notice the door was open, so went in and killed Chuck. That presents a couple of problems."

She nodded. "The first is that, as we said, it makes the killing opportunistic, while the way he was killed, and the fact that nothing was stolen, suggests that the killing was motivated by rage, hatred, revenge, something of that sort."

"Yeah, and the other thing is that"—I shook my head—"Chuck was not a small guy. He was in his thirties and strong, but there is no indication that there was any kind of fight or struggle. Even if you allow that a random man was passing who had a random compulsion to kill, who happened to have a knife with him and happened to see the French windows open, *and* went in, not knowing who the hell was in there, why the hell didn't Chuck defend himself?"

She scratched her cheek and looked away at the road, like she was trying to see the random guy with a knife. "Yeah," she said. "Random killer or not, that's a problem that is going to keep coming up. For now let's say that we discard the random passerby, and we go with the second option. Somebody has some kind of grudge against Chuck. They have been watching him, even stalking him."

I took a couple of steps back toward her, nodding. "So he is already armed. He has chosen a knife rather than a gun."

"Yeah, because he wants to make it a silent kill, but also, it is more personal this way."

I frowned. "Mm-hm, it is very personal, and also, this keeps nagging at me, Dehan, the *location* of the wounds." I took her arm by the wrist and lifted it with my left hand, pointing at her armpit and the inside of her biceps as I did so. "Deep cuts into the basilic vein and the brachial artery, on both arms. And then—"

I dropped onto one knee and pushed her right leg slightly to one side, pointing with my right hand to her inside thigh. "He cuts deep into the inside thigh, into the femoral artery, the femoral vein, and the saphenous . . ."

"You having fun down there, Stone?"

I looked up at her and smiled. "Try to stay on task, Dehan." I got to my feet. "Again, in *both* legs. And while he's doing this,

Chuck is passive, not fighting back. This guy was either some kind of ninja, or Chuck was drugged."

Dehan was squinting at me and lowered her shades over her eyes against the bright sun. "They must have done a tox. What did it say?"

I shook my head. "Nothing. No drugs were found in his system."

She turned and stepped back into the house. I followed.

"Killer comes in," I said. "Does he meet Chuck down here? Do they talk? If they do, whatever they talk about leads them upstairs..."

"But *not*..." She turned to face me. "... as you would expect, to the office. It leads them to the bedroom."

I grunted. "Where the killer pulls a knife and, within a fraction of a second, incapacitates Chuck, throws him on the bed, and goes to work on his arteries. This is impossible. It's insane."

"But it gets better, Stone." She walked away from me, toward the stairs, with her hands on her hips, then turned and walked back, telling me how it got better.

"Because, with the killer on his way down the stairs, or right there, with him, Chuck then calls his wife, *six times*. And when she doesn't answer, he calls 911. Now, he has to be damn quick." She pointed up at the bedroom, like she wanted me to see what was going on up there in her mind. "Because he is bleeding out fast. So either the killer *was* a damn ninja, did his work super fast and left..."

"Or he was still there when Chuck was making the calls..."

"And that is really disturbing."

"It's disturbing and makes as little sense as the rest of it." I paused, searching my mind for images that made sense, trying to make movies in my mind of a sequence of events that was logical and coherent. "What would his purpose be?"

"To draw her home. So perhaps she was also a target."

"But she didn't come. She said she saw half a dozen missed calls. They were talking, and she didn't hear the phone."

"So time passes, the killer panics and runs, and that's when he calls 911, just before losing consciousness and dying."

"And just before his wife gets home."

"She and the killer must have just missed each other by seconds."

I grunted. "And he never came back." I sighed loudly and ran my fingers through my hair. "That doesn't make sense either. If she was part of the target, why did he wait for her to leave, and why didn't he come back? And that brings us to the final thing that is playing on my mind, Dehan."

"I know." She reached behind her neck and tied her long, black hair into a knot. It was a gesture that never failed to distract me. "I know," she said again. "At this point, the killer, having severed the main arteries and veins in Chuck's body, having saturated the whole bed and the carpet in blood, walks out without leaving a single bloody footprint, a single handprint, not a single drop of blood in the house except the blood in the bedroom."

I shrugged. "How'd he do that? He cuts Chuck to pieces in seconds, waits a couple of minutes or less while he makes his calls, then exits without leaving a trace. Even if we said that he went into the bathroom and showered, which is in itself insane, where are the footprints across the floor? Did he mop those up too? And how long did it take him? Because he has a few minutes tops for Chuck to make his calls and bleed out before Angela gets home. And in that time he showered, changed his clothes, put the damp towel in the laundry basket, mopped the floor . . . How did he do that?"

She was quiet for a long while. I wandered to the kitchen and stood in the doorway for a moment, looking out through the window at the backyard. Over my shoulder I heard Dehan say, "He has some serious skills."

I found myself nodding absently as my eyes traveled below and to the left of the sink. There was the washing machine. I could see the folded shapes of clothes within, dark with mold. She had washed clothes that day, and never bothered to take them out.

"What are you staring at?"

She rested her chin on my shoulder. I gestured at the washing machine, then went and opened the dishwasher. All the cutlery, plates, pots, and pans from their last meal together were there.

"She may as well have come back," said Dehan.

I stood and looked at her. "What do you mean?"

She met my eye. "He destroyed her life as completely as though he had stabbed her in the heart."

"Yeah."

I found the pantry, and inside it I found a roll of garden refuse sacks. I peeled one off, hunkered down, and pulled all the moldy clothes out of the washing machine. The stench of stale detergent was about as bad as the smell of dead rats upstairs. I sealed the bag and stood for a moment. Dehan was frowning at me.

"What are you thinking?"

"I don't know. But something is wrong." I pulled out my cell and called Joe at the lab.

"Stone, how you doing? What's on your mind?"

"You remember the Inglewood case, about two years ago?"

"Nope. Should I?"

"It was an odd case, guy stabbed to death in his house, deep cuts to the insides of his thighs and arms. I thought you might remember. Anyway, listen, I'm at the house. It hasn't been touched since the murder. The bloody sheets are still on the bed. There are things, Joe, that just don't make sense to me. At the time, as far as I can see, no thorough inspection was made of the en suite bathroom upstairs. I guess there didn't seem to be a need. But, I'd like you to send a team and just go over that bathroom with a fine-tooth comb. Look for everything from prints to traces of blood, especially in the bath, but on the walls, tiles, floor . . . everywhere."

"Sure, give me the address. I'll send a team over right away."

"Thanks, and Joe? For the sake of completeness, take the sheets too. See what you can get from them."

I gave him the address and hung up. Dehan shrugged at me.

"I get it, but you're wasting your time. He didn't have time. It's that simple."

I shrugged back. "Where is the blood?"

CHAPTER 3

I handed the house keys, and the bag of moldy washing, over to Joe and his crew, then strolled down to Mrs. Nowak to explain that we would be hanging on to the keys. She scowled at us through the half-open door and snarled, "I never went in there, see? I never put pawee-son down neither. That ain't my place to do that. Though there was rats enough to do it! God only knows!"

We assured her it had never crossed our minds, and we left her peering darkly through the crack in her door as we returned to the car. When we got there, I leaned on the roof and felt the heat seep through my jacket and into my arms. It was somehow reassuring. Dehan stood across from me.

"What now, big guy?"

"Now?" I looked up at the dappled green leaves of the chestnuts. "Now I could use a beer to wash away the smell of those rats. But first I think we go and talk to Angela Inglewood. Then we'll have some lunch and mull this over." I opened the door and stopped halfway in. "There is something very wrong with this, Dehan. Something's very wrong, and it ain't right."

We climbed in and slammed the doors, the cat growled, and we pulled away toward the Cross Bronx Expressway. It was a short drive, and at Pennyfield Avenue we took the exit and went down as far as Chaffee Avenue, a short cul-de-sac overlooking the Locust Point Marina. Angela Inglewood's house was one but last from the end, on the left.

It was a massive, double-fronted redbrick affair that looked mock-Georgian, with a Palladian, stucco portico and gabled dormers jutting out of the attic. A hedged path traversed the front lawn to six steps that ascended to the front door. I glanced at Dehan and, in silence, we made our way through the front yard.

Angela Inglewood opened the door almost immediately. She was a tall woman, almost six foot, slim and boney, with very white skin and very black hair pulled back into a severe bun at the base of her skull. Her eyes were a deep blue, and though they spoke of sympathy and kindness, her lips were tight and thin and told of a compassion that had withered into caution through lack of reciprocity from a world that didn't care.

She said, "You must be the detectives," like that was exactly the kind of thing she would expect from us.

We showed her our badges. "I am John Stone; this is my partner, Detective Dehan."

"You'd better come in."

She stood back, and we went into an old-fashioned hall where a mahogany staircase climbed to upper floors over a large, Spanish credenza, and heavy wooden doors opened to left and right into rooms you just knew she called parlors, where there were doilies on the chairs, coasters on the occasional tables, and the furniture had "do not disturb" signs on it.

She gestured us to the door on my right, and we followed her through it into a cozy room overcrowded with furniture that was pretending to be antique. The bookshelves had little room for books, because the space was taken up with small statues of kittens and milkmaids, and one of a humorously drunk Irishman leaning against a lamppost. You could tell he was Irish by his green hat.

She sat on the sofa, with her back to the window, and we each took an armchair. I drew breath to speak, trying to organize my thoughts, but she spoke first.

"You have seen the house now. I honestly don't know what you can hope to have found that the initial investigation missed." She shook her head. "I don't know what you hope I can tell you."

I let out the breath I'd drawn in as a small sigh.

"*I* don't honestly know, Mrs. Inglewood. But there are a few things that don't make a lot of sense to us at the moment."

She gave a laugh that was on the bitter side of harsh. "Sense? Does *any* of it make sense? A man is murdered in his own home, in broad daylight, in the middle of the afternoon! Nothing is stolen, nothing is taken, there is no apparent reason for the killing, and you are looking for sense?"

Dehan leaned forward with her elbows on her knees and her hands clasped.

"Mrs. Inglewood, my partner and I have been working homicide for many years. Between us we have racked up about thirty-five years of experience. You can imagine how many murders we have seen in that time."

Angela Inglewood looked momentarily chastened and averted her eyes. "A good few, I should imagine," she said.

Dehan nodded. "Yeah, a good few. A few of them, mainly those that are gang related, make a kind of sordid, brutal sense to the killers and to the victims, the pursuit of power or money. But the vast majority make no sense at all to anyone in their right minds. They make sense to the killer, and they have a twisted logic to people like my partner and me, who have learned over the years to understand the way these people's minds work. We don't think of it in terms of sense, or logic or sanity. We think in terms of motive."

Angela stared at her for a while, then her eyes shifted to me. I said, "We can't find anything that remotely suggests a motive in this case. But more than that, there are a number of facts that don't seem to fit into any kind of explanation for what happened. I am not going to trouble you with them now—I know how distressing it must be for you to have all this dragged up again—but I am going to ask you to try and think back. Was there anybody, anybody at all, who might have wished your husband harm? Who might have wanted to hurt him?"

Her expression was one of helplessness, shaking her head. "No! No, not at all. I won't say that everybody loved Chuck. They didn't. But nobody hated him either. Nobody even disliked him. He was a normal man. He worked hard, he had a bit of a temper, but he was . . ." She shrugged and spread her hands. It was a gesture of resignation. "He was just *unremarkable*. I guess that would be the word. That's why it's so senseless. I loved him because he was a hardworking man who cared deeply about his family. We couldn't have kids. We found that out early on. But he did everything he could for us."

"What about in business? Did he ever cross anyone, make an enemy, borrow from a loan shark . . . ?"

For a moment her face lit up with amusement, and for a second it was a nice face, pretty and humorous. She laughed. "Chuck? No! He never borrowed. 'You don't pay money for money,' he used to say. And as for making enemies, that wasn't the way he *did* business. He did business by cultivating loyal friends. If he did business with you, he made damn sure you were happy. But if he didn't get his pound of flesh, if he wasn't happy with you, he never did business with you again. That was the end of it." She trailed off, gazing down at her hands neatly laid in her lap. "So to answer your questions, no. He had no enemies. He didn't have great friends—there wasn't a huge turnout at his funeral—but nobody hated Chuck. Not many people really loved him either, but those who knew him well respected him."

We were silent for a while, Angela looking down at her hands, Dehan watching her. I sighed, and it sounded loud in that gloomy room.

"Mrs. Inglewood, I am sorry, but I have to ask you this." She looked up to meet my gaze, and her eyes were startlingly blue and intense. "Was there another man?"

She immediately sat up straight, squaring her shoulders. I held up my hands, placating. She said, "How dare you!"

"I don't mean at the same time..."

Dehan stepped in. "What Detective Stone means is, was there ever, at any time, another man?"

"Certainly not!"

"Mrs. Inglewood," Dehan persisted. "Think before you answer. You are an attractive woman." Angela looked startled. Dehan ignored her. "Is it possible: an old boyfriend, a suitor, even someone you turned away...?"

Angela shook her head, but there was something uncertain in the gesture. Something about the way she knit her brow suggested the question confused her, like the thought had never occurred to her before.

"No... Men have never..." She left the statement unfinished and instead said, "Chuck was the only man in my life. There was never anybody else."

"You see..." I hesitated, and she watched me. Her eyes said she didn't like my questions, and she didn't like me any better. Dehan stepped in again.

"Mrs. Inglewood, we think that the original investigation may have foundered partly because they missed a key point."

Angela's blue eyes shifted back to Dehan. "What point?"

"That your husband was not the sole, intended victim."

"*What?*"

"We think, for reasons we really don't want to go into right now, that you were intended to return while the killer was there."

Her skin, already pale, turned ghostly. "The phone calls."

Dehan nodded. "Yes, the phone calls. We think they were intended to lure you home. Which would suggest that your husband's death might have been intended in some way as a punishment for you."

Her voice was barely a whisper. "That's insane."

I spoke quietly. "I don't want to go into the details, but whichever way you look at it, there is no escaping the fact that the killer's behavior is hard to explain unless he intended you to be there."

Her eyes went wide. "Why?"

"Because he must have been there while your husband was trying to call you. He must have watched him do it, and allowed it. And that must mean, perforce, that in some way, somehow, you have some kind of connection or relationship with the killer, even if you are not immediately aware of it."

"That's . . ." She trailed off. "That's not possible. No. I can't believe that."

"You need to think, Mrs. Inglewood. Don't try to answer it now, but think about it."

She stood and clasped her hands in front of her, like two hooks linked across her belly. She walked to the window but didn't look out at the silent trees in the afternoon. She stared instead, unseeing, down at the windowsill. I gave her a while and then spoke.

"There is something else, Mrs. Inglewood."

"Something else? This isn't enough?"

"What kind of relationship did you and your husband have with your niece, Sadie?"

She screwed up her brow hard at the windowsill before turning to look at me.

"Sadie?" I waited. Dehan watched her, curious. "Relationship? She was our niece. She lived across the way. What kind of relationship . . . ?" She shrugged. "I don't know what you're getting at?"

"Were you fond of her? Did she visit often?"

She turned toward us now, with her back to the bright glass. Her face was cast in deep shadow so her expression was invisible.

"Of course. She was our niece. My sister lived on the next street. We visited often, and they visited us. Why are you asking about Sadie?"

"Sadie was raped."

"Yes. I know."

"A few months before your husband was murdered."

"Almost a year before."

"It is a big coincidence."

"You can't possibly think . . ." She couldn't say the words, so she said, "What are you suggesting?"

Dehan answered. "We're not suggesting anything, Mrs. Inglewood. But we have to wonder whether the two incidents aren't connected. Whatever the truth may be, is it possible that somebody got it into their head that your husband raped Sadie? After all, she refused to name her rapist, or even say where and when it had happened. Could this have been revenge?"

She stared around the floor, searching, as though she might find that absurd person there and give them the sharp end of her tongue. "Who?" she said. "Who could think that?"

I said, "We're not suggesting it, Mrs. Inglewood. We are just asking if it is possible. A boyfriend, even your brother-in-law . . ."

"No!" She shook her head violently, not looking at us. "No, no, no! What you are suggesting is insane! You are . . ." She faltered, searching for a word strong enough. ". . . *completely* wrong, on the wrong track, wrong! Patrick is a good, kind man. Sadie was a normal teenager. Her friends were just normal kids. This *thing* you are suggesting is just *wrong*!"

"Okay." I stood. "Mrs. Inglewood, we are very sorry to have distressed you. All we want is to find who did this to Chuck."

At the sound of his name she froze and stared up into my face. I went on.

"Whoever did it is a very sick person, who may have wanted to harm you too, so we are going to leave no stone unturned searching for them." I smiled at her, spoke quietly. "If you'll forgive me for taxing the metaphor, turning some of those stones has to be painful. But we have to do it. It is one hell of a coincidence, that both of these things should happen within a few months of each other." I nodded. "And it may be just that, a coincidence. But it also may be that somebody, for some reason, believed that Chuck had raped Sadie. And we have to explore that possibility. So you need to think about that. You need to think about who, in your circle of family, friends, and wider acquaintances, might have had a grudge against Chuck. Possibly somebody who was close to Sadie. Can you do that for us?"

She had become more calm as I spoke to her. Now she nodded, once, slowly, then a couple of times more quickly, as though she had come to some decision.

"Yes, I'll do that. I'm sorry. It is all so fresh. He was my rock, my pillar. He took care of me, of everything. And . . ."

She shook her head, then seemed to crumple onto the sofa. Her pretty, white face became pink and distorted, shiny with a sudden discharge of tears. Dehan sat next to her and put her arms around her. She tried to talk, but all that came out were distorted, twisted sounds, until she buried her face in Dehan's shoulder and clung to her.

I sat.

After a few minutes her convulsive crying stopped, her breathing steadied, and she pulled away from Dehan. I handed her a handkerchief, which she took, blew her nose, and dabbed her eyes.

"I'm sorry," she said again. "I still have trouble accepting that he's gone."

"I'm so sorry we have to . . ." I shrugged and spread my hands.

She shook her head. "It has to be done. I'll do my best to think about what you've said. I'll talk to Cathy. I'll see if anything occurs to me."

We thanked her, and she showed us out.

Midday had matured into a golden afternoon as we made our way between the hedges to the sidewalk where the Jaguar was parked. Dehan leaned with the heels of her hands on the roof and shook her head, looking at me through dark shades. "Man!" she said. "It doesn't get easier."

"Nope. Pepperoni pizza and beer might take the edge off, though."

"The man has wisdom."

We climbed in, and I sat awhile with the key in my hand, staring at the fringe of trees that marked the end of the cul-de-sac, where the banks ran down to the creek. I didn't see them though. All I could see was the open French windows on the Inglewoods' drive, and a figure stepping in, from the sunlight to the shadows within. An anonymous figure, almost shapeless, who moved silently through the house, up the stairs, and confronted Chuck Inglewood with a very sharp knife.

And cut him. Cut him deeply and cruelly, and left him to bleed to death. And not a drop of that blood stained the killer.

"Stone?"

I turned and looked at Dehan. She had raised her shades on top of her head, like a knight's visor, and she was frowning and smiling at me. I smiled back. "What?"

"Come back. It's lunchtime."

"*Andiamo!*" I said, facetiously, and turned the key in the ignition. "*Andiamo a mangiare la pizza!*"

"Yeah," she said. "What the man said." And we pulled away.

Scan the QR code below to purchase BLEED OUT.
Or go to: righthouse.com/bleed-out

Printed in Dunstable, United Kingdom